PURRFECT DRAGNET

THE MYSTERIES OF MAX 76

NIC SAINT

PURRFECT DRAGNET

The Mysteries of Max 76

Copyright © 2023 by Nic Saint

All rights reserved. No part of this book may be reproduced in any form by any electronic or mechanical means including photocopying, recording, or information storage and retrieval without permission in writing from the author.

This is a work of fiction. Names, characters, places, brands, media, and incidents are either the product of the author's imagination or are used fictitiously. The author acknowledges the trademarked status and trademark owners of various products referenced in this work of fiction, which have been used without permission. The publication/use of these trademarks is not authorized, associated with, or sponsored by the trademark owners.

Edited by Chereese Graves

www.nicsaint.com

Give feedback on the book at: info@nicsaint.com

facebook.com/nicsaintauthor
@nicsaintauthor

First Edition

Printed in the U.S.A

PURRFECT DRAGNET

Just the facts, ma'am

It isn't often that tragedy strikes close to home, but when Charlene Butterwick was kidnapped, that got all of our attention. Snatched in broad daylight in front of Town Hall, it wasn't long before the entire Hampton Cove police force organized a dragnet and went all out to find the mayor. And since in a sense Charlene is our mayor also, as well as our human's aunt by marriage, we volunteered for the search. It soon transpired that whoever was behind this spectacular abduction had also been involved in a home invasion gone wrong, with the homeowner not having survived his ordeal. So it wasn't too much to say that the pressure was on to find Charlene before it was too late.

CHAPTER 1

Dooley had been wandering the streets and backstreets of his neighborhood, looking for a very specific thing. So far, he hadn't found it yet, but since he was determined to keep on looking until he had, he was reasonably optimistic that eventually he would hit upon the perfect birthday gift for his best friend and housemate Max. It hadn't occurred to him that Max's birthday was fast approaching until Harriet had mentioned it casually in a conversation they were having on an unrelated topic. She claimed that she had already secured the perfect gift for their voluminous blorange friend and that Max would be so happy.

It was then that it dawned on Dooley that he hadn't gotten Max a gift at all. In fact, he had totally forgotten that his friend's birthday was coming up. Even Brutus said he had already gotten his gift, and even though it wasn't possibly as nice as Harriet's—tough to compete with the Persian feline—it was something that Max would love.

At that point, they had both turned to Dooley, eager to

learn what he had gotten for Max, and he had to admit he'd totally forgotten about the happy occasion.

"You're not serious," said Harriet, looking aghast. "You forgot about Max's birthday? But Dooley!"

"Yeah, that's a grave oversight if ever there was one," Brutus had grunted, looking equally surprised.

And so Dooley had suddenly felt like one of those things that you find under a rock when it's turned over: very low indeed! And so he had pledged a solemn oath right then and there that he wouldn't rest until he had found his friend the best present ever. The problem was: what do you give a cat who has everything? Also: as a rule, cats aren't big on the kind of paraphernalia humans like to surround themselves with, or the accoutrements of a consumerist society. So no sports cars or jacuzzis or diamond rings or fancy clothes. Not even a new cologne purportedly created by a well-known celebrity or the latest gizmo to be touted on social media.

Cats are fairly simple creatures, so for the life of him, for a long while, he simply couldn't think of what to give his friend. But then suddenly inspiration struck, and he thought he had it. The gift to end all gifts. The one thing that Max craved above all else: a pipe! After all, Max was a great detective, and as far as Dooley could tell, all great detectives smoked a pipe, or at least they did in the olden days. The problem was: where was he going to find such a super-duper pipe? And especially the very specific pipe he had in mind for his friend: the original pipe that used to belong to that other great detective, Sherlock Holmes.

And so the long quest had begun, with Dooley hunting high and low for Mr. Holmes's pipe. One thing was for sure: a great man like Sherlock Holmes presumably owned several pipes, so he wouldn't mind giving one as a gift to an esteemed colleague like Max. At least that's what Dooley hoped would be the case. But first he had to locate Mr. Holmes, and then he had to induce that great man to part with one of his pipes. It hadn't to be *the* pipe, of course. Any old pipe would do, as long as it belonged to the legendary detective. And then Max could put it in his mouth and really look the part. He might even add a deerstalker hat.

Gone would be the snickers by some denizens of Hampton Cove when confronted with the latest sample of Max's brilliance. Finally, he'd get the recognition he deserved. And Dooley had been scouring the neighborhood in search of the house where Mr. Holmes lived, when he thought he had finally found it: a ramshackle old building that had nevertheless retained some of its former glorious splendor. This must be where the detective lived, he just knew it.

After a hopeful glance at the house, which stood back from the street and was fronted by a patch of front yard that looked about as derelict as the house itself, he stepped through the wrought-iron fence that hung crooked and forlorn on its hinges like a drunken sailor and with a touch of trepidation set a course for the main house. It didn't look all that welcoming, but that was simply the facade, he knew. Once inside, the panorama that would spread out before him would be that of the comfortable and pleasant dwelling as inhabited by Mr. Holmes and his good friend Dr. Watson, and as lovingly attended to by Mrs. Hudson.

For a moment, he wondered how to proceed, but then he saw that a small window was ajar next to the front door, and so he deftly jumped up onto the windowsill and took a curious peek inside. The room was dark, but that was fine. It didn't take long for his trained cat eyes to get an overview of the situation, and he wasn't disappointed when he discovered that the inside of the house was indeed much more accommodating than the outside indicated. Clearly, the great detective liked to present a different face to the world than his actual dwelling evidenced. Subterfuge, a weapon employed by all the great detectives.

Even Max had perfected this particular device: at first glance, he looked like a rather oversized and overweight red cat, but underneath that facade lurked a brain as formidable if not more formidable than that of his human counterparts in the field of private detecting. Mr. Holmes, Mr. Poirot, Miss Marple, Mr. Mason, all of them could take his correspondence course and learn a thing or two or three.

What he didn't see was either the detective himself, seated in a comfortable armchair as he had envisioned, discussing a recent case with his friend and loyal sidekick Mr. Watson, or the detective's collection of pipes. But that didn't deter him. Instead, he decided to slip inside and go in search of the owner and proprietor or, if Mr. Holmes was out on a case, at least Mrs. Hudson, no doubt busy in the kitchen or in the greenhouse attending to Mr. Holmes's orchids. Though he could be thinking about a different detective.

He slipped gracefully down from the windowsill and found himself on a nice hardwood floor, and as he moved stealthily to the door, then opened it by giving it a gentle push with his head, the hallway stretched out before him, just as nicely and neatly furnished as the room he had just left. Mahogany furniture, waxed hardwood floors, paintings of bucolic country life scenes on the walls as well as polished wall sconces—clearly, Mr. Holmes's detecting work paid dividends.

Which reminded him that maybe Max should start charging for his own services as well. Until now, he had always worked on a strictly pro bono basis, but after solving so many cases, perhaps it wasn't a bad idea to put things on a firm business footing from now on. Rent an office, hire a secretary, advertise in the paper and online. Do things the way they should be done. After all, Max deserved it, and no one works for free, so why should he?

He glanced briefly at the staircase leading up to the next floor and wondered why the house was so eerily quiet. Unless, of course, business had taken its inhabitants to a different continent. Europe, maybe, or Asia, or even Africa. A great detective's work is never done, and the demands on his time are many and varied, from all corners of the globe.

And he had just taken a peek into the next room when he saw something that his young eyes found very hard to interpret—at least at first.

A man sat in the semi-darkness, tied to a chair, and didn't look all that comfortable. It was difficult to make out his features, for someone had pulled a bag over his head. In front of him stood another man who was wearing a mask and who was saying something along the lines of, "And now you're going to tell me where you stashed that painting, old man, or I'll be forced to become very unpleasant—and I'm not even kidding!"

For a moment, Dooley wondered if either of these two men could be Sherlock Holmes, but then he figured probably not. Mr. Holmes would never get involved in anything as base as robbing another person, as this man clearly seemed to be in the process of doing. Then again, it could be all part of some kind of elaborate stage play. An experiment to limber up the mind and prepare one's reflexes for any contingency. But try as he might, he simply couldn't see it. And so he decided to take his leave and let these people get on with whatever they were doing.

The last thing he heard, before he retreated back into the safety of the hallway, was that the man with the bag over his head said, in a sort of plaintive voice: "But I don't have any paintings! You must have me mistaken for somebody else!"

"Then I'm afraid you leave me no choice but to hurt you something bad!"

Which is when Dooley realized that perhaps it was time to go and get the assistance of that other person who played such an integral part in the world of Sherlock Holmes: Inspector Lestrade. And so he hurried out of the hallway, into the room, out through the window, and was going at a fast clip with but a single goal in mind: make sure that the police arrived before that poor old man was subjected any longer to the treatment his tormentor was dishing out.

All in all, it looked as if Max wouldn't get Sherlock's pipe for his birthday after all.

CHAPTER 2

Roger Turton took another sip from his iced tea as he looked out of the window of the high-rise where his fancy new apartment was located. He had only moved in about a week or six ago, and so it still felt very new to him, even the smell was still that of a new building that still has to settle. Roger's wife had done the decorating without any input from her husband at all, since frankly he couldn't be bothered, and also, according to most who knew him, he didn't have an artistic bone in his body.

As a chef, his thing was food and cooking for large numbers of people, making sure they left his restaurant happy and satisfied was what drove him in life. So much so that he didn't really care whether he lived in a ramshackle old house or a fancy new condo like the one they had moved into.

A cry of distress brought him out of his reverie, and he looked up to find his three-year-old daughter standing behind him, clutching the sofa and holding a toy plush bear in her chubby hand, handing it to him. For some indiscernible reason, the bear was missing its head. As he took the plush animal and went in search of the head to reattach it by applying some of his magical parental powers, he found that the apartment was otherwise curiously devoid of life.

"Kirsten?" he called out, wondering where his wife could be. She had promised to look after Quinnie while he was busy creating new recipes for the restaurant, a thriving business now in its second year and still going from strength to strength.

When no response came, he went in search of her, figuring she might have stepped out of the apartment for a moment to run an errand. But when he found her phone on the kitchen island, as well as her keys, a sudden niggle of concern entered his mind. And so it was with an urgency in his step that he quickly searched the rest of the spacious condo for a sign of his wife, but in vain.

Quinnie, who had toddled after him, still eager to see her bear restored to its former glory, now held out her arms, so he picked her up and hoisted her onto his arm while he fought against his tendency to think up the worst scenarios for what could have happened to Kirsten. So when the door suddenly swung open and his wife of fifteen years walked in, looking as fresh and bright and happy as usual, he heaved a sigh of intense relief.

"Where did you go?" he asked, trying his utmost to hide his distress.

"The postman rang the door downstairs," she said. "A package arrived. Didn't you hear me?"

He shook his head. So lost in his own world had he been that of course he hadn't heard a thing. Kirsten took Quinnie from him and gave him a light pat on the cheek. "Wake up, honey. The world is calling."

"What about the package?" he asked when he saw that Kirsten's hands were conspicuously empty of a package of any description.

"Oh, turns out it wasn't for us but for Jackie."

"Oh," he said, wondering how the mailman could have a problem distinguishing between Kirsten Turton and Jackie Parker as they lived on different floors. He studied his wife for a moment, but when he saw no sign of subterfuge, he decided to let it go. He was starting to get paranoid in his old age, and so he forced his mind to return to the problem at hand: what was he going to do for Christmas and New Year this year? It had to be something to top last year's sold-out bash. And that was exactly the problem: it wasn't enough to be successful. Both his customers and the food critics expected him to go from strength to strength and to top last year's knock-out success with this year's even greater smash. If you're not moving forward, you're moving backward and all of that. Which sometimes made him wonder how long he'd be able to go on like this.

But then he dispelled the unsettling thought and sat down at the kitchen counter and started to jot down some ideas. He had a family to support, after all, not to mention a substantial mortgage to pay. So there was no room for second-guessing or doubt. Onward and upward. And he had just written down a possible idea when a tug at his pants leg had him look down.

It was Quinnie, and as she thrust her headless bear into his hands once again, she gave him a look of annoyance. It wasn't hard to know what she was thinking: 'Fix it, Daddy! Fix it now!'

He might be Hampton Cove's hottest chef, but first and foremost he was a father, and fathers have to put their little princesses first. And rightly so.

And as he renewed his search for the poor bear's head, looking underneath the sofa, he noticed how Kirsten was texting, a slight smile playing about her lips, and once again that annoying feeling of worry started niggling at him. The feeling that there was something she wasn't telling him. That she was harboring some kind of secret. But when she noticed him studying her, she gave him the kind of dazzling smile that had made him fall in love with her in the first place, and he parked his doubts and grabbed the head of Papa Bear from underneath the couch where it had rolled, and wondered how he was going to get it attached to its parent body once again.

CHAPTER 3

Sonny Hayworth looked left, then right, before grabbing the bottle of olive oil from the shelf and stuffing it into his pocket. Then he walked along as if nothing had happened. A glance had already told him that Wilbur Vickery, the owner of the General Store, wasn't at the checkout counter as usual. Instead, he was talking to another customer in a different part of the store. So Sonny felt pretty relaxed about his initiative. So relaxed, in fact, that he decided to push his luck and go for the gold. He had olive oil, tomato sauce, sundried tomatoes, capers, pesto, herbs and spices, spaghetti, ground beef... Now all he needed was some Parmesan, and tonight he'd be able to create a feast unlike any he'd made in recent times.

And so he headed over to the dairy section, found what he was looking for, and quick as a flash, grabbed a big block of Parmesan and stuffed it into yet another one of the many pockets this special coat of his concealed. If you saw him, you wouldn't know that he'd already purloined several items of merchandise. That was because he was good and had been trained by the very best.

His dad had been a pickpocket, his mom a con artist, and his granddad, famously so, had been the person who had actually stolen the President's satellite phone when the man had paid a visit to Long Island back in the eighties. Unfortunately, Granddad Hayworth had been caught at the time, but the story had entered family lore and was still being told at family dinners to this day.

If Granddad had still been alive, nowadays he would be stealing mobile phones, of course, since those bulky satellite phones had gone the way of the dodo. And Sonny was walking to the exit, hoping for a clean getaway, when he was suddenly waylaid by the fat cat that Wilbur insisted on keeping. The cat had taken up a position squarely in the center of the health and beauty aisle and now let out a loud lament that caused all those in the store to pop their heads up from their various vantage points in other aisles to see what was going on.

"Shut up, fatso," Sonny hissed viciously.

But the cat wouldn't shut up. Instead, he kept on wailing away, producing a very annoying sound of the kind that only cats can make—a sound so terrifying that Sonny could feel his innards twisting and turning in agony at the sheer sense of discomfort it provoked in him.

Before long, Wilbur came hurrying up, took one look at Sonny, and crossed his arms in front of his chest. "Take off your coat," the shopkeeper demanded.

"What? Why?" said Sonny.

"Because I said so, that's why. Take it off!"

And even though he protested that this was an infringement on his human rights and threatened to go to court and file a harassment suit against the man, in the end he was forced to comply. Out came the Parmesan, the tomato sauce, the spaghetti of the angel hair variety, the olive oil, the sundried tomatoes, capers, pesto, herbs and spices, ground beef, and even the six-pack of brewskis he'd tucked away, along with the diet Pepsi for his cousin Bertie.

"I'm calling the cops," said Wilbur.

"Don't call the cops," he suggested.

"Oh, I'm calling them," said the shop owner. "This isn't the first time you've stolen from me, Sonny, and frankly I'm sick and tired of your nonsense." As he took out his phone, Sonny thought frantically about how to avert disaster.

And that's when he said something he probably shouldn't have said. It certainly wasn't something his dad would have said, or his granddad—hardy men as they both were, steeped in crime and immune to the slings and arrows of law enforcement or irate shop owners. "If you don't call the cops, I'll make it worth your while," he blurted out.

Wilbur, who had put on his reading glasses, looked up. "And how do you propose to do that, huh? Seems to me you ain't got two nickels to rub together."

"I've got some information for you that you will find very interesting," he said. He was already regretting his statement, but it was too late now. And besides, it wasn't as if it was such a big deal. Not to him, at least.

"And what's that?" asked Wilbur, a keen look having stolen over his face.

"What if I tell you that Mayor Butterwick is about to be kidnapped?"

Wilbur frowned. "Charlene? Now who in their right mind would go and do a crazy thing like that?"

"Her ex-husband," said Sonny. "He wants her back, and he's willing to go to any length to make it happen, even kidnap. And that's not all."

"It's not?"

"He's also going to try and get rid of her current husband."

"Chief Lip? You gotta be joking."

He shook his head. "I'm not. I've got it from a reliable source. Everything has been arranged and will go down soon. Very soon." He swallowed. "So what do you say, Vickery? Is that information worth the price of a piece of cheese and some measly ingredients for the perfect pasta I was gonna cook for my daughter?"

Wilbur's expression softened. "Look, I know you've hit on hard times, Sonny. But that doesn't mean you should go and rob people. I also have bills to pay, you know, same as you. What if I were to hold up a gas station because I have a hard time paying for gas? Huh? It wouldn't be a nice thing if we all thought like you."

"I know," he said, feeling utterly embarrassed. Not about the fact that he was a thief, since that was his profession, after all, but that he was such a lousy thief that he'd gone and allowed himself to get caught. "So we good?"

Wilbur hesitated. "When is this supposed to go down?"

"Soon," he said. "That's all I know."

"Okay, fine," said Wilbur. "Clear out."

He started grabbing the wares he had stolen, but Wilbur quickly made it clear that he wasn't going to let him make a nice Parmesan pasta for his daughter that night—unless he paid for it.

And since what the shopkeeper had said was certainly true, and he couldn't necessarily afford to pay for the ingredients of the feast himself, he gave the man a nod and walked off.

He just hoped that no one would find out about his run-in with the General Store's cat and owner—or he'd never hear the end of it. And as he walked out of the store, he removed another piece of Parmesan cheese from the second coat he wore underneath the first one, a bottle of olive oil, tomato sauce, spaghetti of the angel hair variety, sundried tomatoes, capers, pesto, herbs and spices, ground beef, a six-pack of brewskis, a diet Pepsi and a nice big piece of chocolate, of the kind that Kiki adored.

Wilbur might think he was clever, but then he was no match for the one and only Sonny Hayworth, he thought with a smirk. Pasta dinner was a go!

CHAPTER 4

I saw the object sail through the air and crash to the ground with a soft, dull thud. Since I'd been fast asleep, it took me a while to realize what was going on. There were screams all around, of course, and before long, people were crowding around the unfortunate victim of the fall and calling for an ambulance to arrive.

I couldn't exactly see what was happening due to all the people surrounding him or her, and so for a while I just stared, wondering if what I was seeing was actually happening or if I was still dreaming, as often happens. But then finally, there was a break in the crowd, and I saw that the person lying in the middle of the street was a young woman of familiar aspect, and my concern deepened.

I had seen her walking around the block with her dog, so I knew she lived nearby. Since it's never a pleasant experience to see someone you know, or vaguely know as in this instance, come to any harm, I hoped she would be all right.

The crowd thickened even more as the entire neighborhood seemed to have stepped out into the street. As I watched on, I could already hear the sound of the ambulance approaching, so help mercifully was on the way.

It was only at that moment that I became aware of the absence of my good friend Dooley. When I had closed my eyes for a nice little nap, he had been lying next to me, and now, if you catch my drift, he wasn't.

The two of us had selected the windowsill that offers a nice view of the street outside for our nap, since we had grown tired of all our other spots. After all, how many times can you sleep in the same place? It gets so tedious after a while, and so we like to mix things up by keeping it fresh and exciting for both of us.

Odelia isn't all that happy about it, accusing us of creating a mess all over the place with our presence, which I have to say I find extremely insulting. As if by the mere act of occupying a space, it will suddenly be soiled. Okay, so perhaps a few stray hairs will take a leave of absence and attach themselves to the surface of our new resting place, but that can't be helped. After all, humans shed, don't they? I keep finding long blond hairs that once were firmly attached to Odelia's cranium but are no longer. And I also find long brown hairs that once called Chase's scalp their own before taking the long leap to freedom. So what's the big deal?

I yawned and wondered where my friend could possibly be. I jumped down from my perch, luxuriously stretched myself and strode into the kitchen for a bite to eat, a sip of water, and a visit to my litter box. I had just completed the former but not the latter when all of a sudden, Dooley came storming into the house.

"Max! Max!" he cried in a bid to attract my attention. "A man is being robbed, and he may be Sherlock Holmes or he may not be Sherlock Holmes, I'm not entirely sure, but he's not happy about it so we have to do something!"

"Hold your horses, buddy," I said, wondering if I should forego my visit to the litter box or not. If what Dooley was saying was true, it might be a while before I got another opportunity. So I made an executive decision and entered my litter box, performed a 180-degree turn, and said from the safety of my box, "Now take a deep breath and give me all of that again, starting from the top."

Even though it was clearly hard for him to comply with my instructions, he took a deep, steadying breath and said, "A man is being robbed by another man, and this other man wants something from the first man he doesn't have—the first man, I mean, not the second. I think he might be Sherlock Holmes—the first man, not the second—but since I didn't see any pipes it could have been Dr. Watson." He then held a paw before his mouth. "Oops. I shouldn't have said that. It was supposed to be a surprise."

I frowned, both from the exertion of the business I was attending to and from Dooley's statement. "The fact that he's being robbed is a surprise, or the fact that he doesn't smoke a pipe?" Neither held great meaning to me, but I was simply stalling for time—until I was ready to face the world again. Hey, multitasking is hard!

"Okay, I might as well tell you," he said. "I totally forgot about your birthday, Max. And so when Harriet and Brutus told me that they had gotten you the greatest gift ever..." Once again, he clasped a paw to his face. "I should not have told you that either!"

"Greatest gift ever? Sounds promising," I said. Though, to be honest, I'm not all that precious about my birthday. I don't even enjoy being reminded that I have a birthday coming up. After all, it's not a lot of fun to realize that you've aged another year, even if you have eight more lives to go. "Though I still don't see what all this has to do with that man being robbed."

"I wanted to give you a pipe," he said, giving me a sheepish look. "I mean, Sherlock Holmes is the greatest human detective, and you're without a doubt the greatest feline detective, so I figured you would love to get into piping."

I smiled. "I don't think that's what it's called, but thank you. It's a nice thought."

"And so I figured the best present would be one of Mr. Holmes's actual pipes, of which I'm sure he's got plenty. And so I entered his house, but before I could find his pipes, I saw this person being manhandled by that awful other person. And so I came running here to tell Odelia—but now I can't find her anywhere!"

"Odelia is at work, and so is Chase," I said. I'd concluded my business and now emerged, after covering it with a substantial amount of litter. "And so is Marge, and so is Tex, and so is Gran."

"But we have to do something, Max!" he said. "That poor Mr. Holmes!"

I was fairly convinced that 'poor Mr. Holmes' wasn't Mr. Holmes at all, since the detective was a figment of a writer's extensive imagination, and also, as far as I could ascertain, he lived over a hundred fictitious years ago in a different country far away. But what was also obvious was that Dooley had witnessed a crime in progress, so it behooved us as crime fighters to do something about it.

"We better go and get help," I said. And so to that end we both hurried out through the pet flap in search of someone—anyone—who could give us a helping paw and stop this heinous crime. Unfortunately, the only presence we found was that of Harriet and Brutus, who were lounging underneath the rose bushes, as they often do. But as I had already expected, of our humans, there was not a single trace. And since nobody else speaks our language, we saw no other recourse but to handle this matter ourselves.

"Poor Mr. Holmes," said Dooley as we hurried on while he led the way.

"What happened here?" asked Harriet when she saw the scene on the street.

"Someone fell," I told her. "A young woman who lives in this neighborhood."

"I think I know her," said Brutus when the ebb and flow of humanity momentarily offered us a view of the person still lying on the ground. "She lives one street over and owns a dog. I've talked to her a couple of times. She's nice."

"Who, the dog or the human?" asked Harriet.

"Well, the dog, of course," said Brutus. "Since humans can't talk to us, except those that belong to a certain bloodline."

"Right," said Harriet. For some reason, she seemed a little out of it, I thought. But since we didn't have time to get into all of that, we followed our friend as he traversed the different streets comprising our neighborhood and before long found ourselves looking up at a house that had seen better days—or years. Or possibly even decades.

"Are you sure that someone lives here?" asked Brutus as he gave the place a dubious look.

"I hope so," said Dooley. "I hope that evil man didn't murder Mr. Holmes!"

"Oh, so you know him, do you?" asked Brutus.

"Of course," said Dooley. "We all know him. Mr. Holmes is only the greatest detective that ever lived."

Brutus gave him an odd look, then shrugged. "Okay, so how do we do this?"

Belatedly, I realized we probably should have asked two of our canine friends to assist us in this delicate matter since they possess both the bark and the bite to scare the living daylights out of any nefarious operator. And as luck would have it, just then Fifi showed up, being walked by her owner Kurt Mayfield.

"Hey, you guys," she said. "What's going on?"

"A man is being attacked in that house over there," I said. "And we're trying to decide what to do about it."

"Oh, no!" said Fifi, who is a Yorkshire Terrier of a most compassionate and humanitarian bent. "What are you waiting for!"

And before Kurt could stop her, she had pulled the leash from his loose grasp and was heading for the front door, barking up a storm all the while.

"Fifi!" Kurt yelled as he went in pursuit of the dog, who had already traversed the unkempt front yard of the house and reached the front door. "Fifi, come back here!"

But Fifi clearly had no intention of coming back. She had discovered that one of the windows was open, and as both we and Kurt looked on, much to our astonishment, she made the jump and moments later had disappeared inside!

"Fifi!" Kurt cried, his voice betraying his sense of panic at seeing his dog going berserk. He then eyed us with a look of less than benevolence. "This is your doing, isn't it?" And before we recovered from this statement, he was running to the house, moments later pursued by the four of us.

"I hope he can save Mr. Holmes," said Dooley, panting a little from the exertion.

Kurt stood pounding on the front door. "Hey, my dog is in there!" he shouted. But when no response came, he finally overcame the natural aversion most humans feel about entering another person's private property in a manner that might be frowned upon by the constabulary, and climbed up onto the window, pushed it open further, and entered the house.

"Let's go!" Dooley said when we hesitated for a moment.

And then he showed us how it was done by following in Fifi and Kurt's path and jumping up and disappearing inside the house.

"I know I'm going to regret this," Brutus grumbled, but finally followed suit, and so did Harriet and I.

"What do you think of my hair, Max?" Harriet asked as she made the jump. "Do you think I should get curls? Or is it better flat like this?"

I gave her an odd look, but was saved having to answer her when we came upon a curious scene: Kurt Mayfield had disappeared from the room where we found ourselves, but not so Brutus, who stood growling near the door.

"I sense evil, Max," he told me. "And I'm not sure if we shouldn't try and escape before it catches us!"

But since the others had all gone before, and I felt we couldn't abort our mission before it was well underway, I decided to take note of Brutus's premonitions and proceed regardless.

"Don't say I didn't warn you," he said as I pushed ahead.

The three of us carefully moved into the hallway, which was as creepy as the facade of the house had indicated, only a lot better maintained. We saw Kurt Mayfield staring at something a little further down the corridor, alongside Fifi, who had stopped yapping and had placed herself on the floor, clearly in the throes of a powerful emotion. Next to them, Dooley stood, a sad sort of look in his eyes.

"Mr. Sherlock Holmes... is dead," he told us as we approached.

We joined the others, and as we did, we found ourselves confronted with a scene that wasn't all that pleasant: on the carpet, a man lay, and from the way he was staring at us with unseeing eyes, it was clear that the force of life that had once inhabited him had fled to yonder shores.

"I know who did it," said Dooley, pulling himself together with a powerful effort.

"You do?" I asked. That was quick.

"It was Professor Moriarty."

CHAPTER 5

Roger Turton stood whipping up a pancake in his state-of-the-art kitchen, located in the best restaurant in town—or at least that's how he felt about it. It had been his life's dream to open his own restaurant, but it had taken many years and a lot of sacrifices before he was finally at a place where he could accomplish this rare feat. Long years as an apprentice and working for other chefs in restaurants across the country and even across the ocean, but finally it all paid off. Though truth be told, he couldn't have done it without the support of his generous backer. If Kirsten's dad hadn't bankrolled the acquisition of the Hungry Pipe from its previous owner Colin Carret, his dream would still be nothing but a mirage.

Kirsten now walked into the kitchen, a frown on her face, and he immediately knew what that meant.

"Another complaint," she told him without prevarication. "They say the sole fillet is still raw."

Now it was his turn to frown. "That's impossible. I've prepared it myself." He glanced over at his sous-chef, who pretended not to be listening but, in actual fact, without a doubt heard every word. Ambitious and talented, Marco Welling wanted to move up in the world of hospitality so badly that his burning ambition sometimes caused friction with his chef—still the boss in his own restaurant.

"Well, they won't eat it," said Kirsten, also darting a quick glance at Marco, then studying her perfectly manicured fingernails. As often happened, she was chewing on a piece of gum, even though he had told her a million times that it gave a horrible impression in front of the guests. When they opened the Hungry Pipe, the division of labor had been clear: he was in charge of the kitchen, and she of the restaurant proper. But sometimes he seriously wondered if he shouldn't have hired a professional manager. But of course, Kirsten's dad wouldn't accept that. One of his stipulations when he bought them the restaurant was that his daughter would be the person the customers would see when they walked in. It was so important to him that he even had it included in the contract that was drawn up when the funds were transferred and the notarized deed was signed.

"Look, just apologize and tell them there must have been a mistake made by the waitstaff," he said, not seeing what else could have happened. "And tell them that their meal is on the house."

"Will do," said Kirsten, not all that interested. She cast another quick glance at Marco and a tiny smile, then left the kitchen to deal with the irate customers.

He wondered if he shouldn't go out there himself and deal with this personally. Customers like to see the chef, especially when they pay a lot of money to sample his food. And since he was the star of the restaurant and the main reason diners flocked there, it was probably a good idea. But when he suggested it to Kirsten, she had put her foot down and reminded him of their respective roles. She wasn't dissuaded when he pointed out that the biggest chefs established a very visible presence in their restaurants. She was the star of the show, and she desperately wanted to keep it that way.

He glanced over at Marco and wondered, not for the first time, if his young sous-chef was harboring ambitions that extended beyond his station. But he couldn't imagine he would purposely send out raw sole fillet just to spite him. His reputation was connected with the Hungry Pipe as much as Roger's was, so he quickly dismissed the thought.

"Well, looks like we'll have to whip up another four plates of our lemon sole," he told Marco.

"No sweat, boss," said the young man. "Four lemon soles coming up."

At least he knew he could trust him to create something delicious every time. In that sense, he reminded Roger a lot of himself at that age: hungry to succeed and extremely willing to learn. If one day Marco opened his own restaurant, which Roger knew he would, he'd look upon his former protégé with pride, just like the chefs at whose feet he had learned all the ins and outs of running a successful kitchen now looked upon him with pride and had sent him cards and gifts when the Hungry Pipe had opened. It felt good to be part of a supportive community.

Shonna, a member of his kitchen staff, now sidled up to him. "I checked that sole fillet myself, boss," she said quietly, stealing a glance at Marco so he wouldn't overhear them. "And I swear that everything was fine with it when it went out."

"I know," he said. "That's what I don't understand." But then he shrugged. "Some customers are like that. They complain in the hope of getting a free meal. As long as it doesn't happen too often, it's fine."

"I guess," she said dubiously. Then she lowered her voice even more. "There's something else I have to tell you, boss."

"Not now, Shonna," he said. The kitchen was buzzing, and now was not the time to lose their focus and let things get out of hand. "Catch me later, when the lunch rush is over, all right?"

She looked disappointed but nodded and returned to her station. She was in charge of the sauces and did an excellent job of it. Another eager student of the art and craft of working in a professional kitchen at a great restaurant, she had joined them from Paris, where she had worked at several other five-star restaurants. Shonna had actually been recommended to him by Chef Laporte, whom Roger had worked for at one time about ten years ago. It was still one of the best and most memorable experiences of his professional life, and he often dreamed of those halcyon years he had spent in the City of Light.

Another wave of orders arrived, and his heart lifted both with the adrenaline the flurry of activity engendered in him and the excitement of seeing his life's dream becoming the huge success he'd always hoped it could be. And so he put the whole business with the disgruntled customers out of his mind and returned to doing what he did best: creating magic by cooking the best meals in the world.

CHAPTER 6

The police had arrived, and also an ambulance, even though it was obvious that the man whose body we found was beyond rescue. Kurt stood outside, talking to a uniformed police officer and giving his statement. The poor guy looked thoroughly discombobulated, I have to say. As a retired music teacher, he probably never had to face these types of contingencies when he was standing in front of his classroom. Regrettably, the four of us have witnessed such scenes frequently in the recent past, so you might say that in a sense we've become a little inured to dealing with this kind of stuff.

Fifi also seemed shocked by what she had seen. It's one thing to dig up and bury bones, but another to find an actual human body. I could have told her that there isn't a lot of difference between finding a bone and finding a human body. The difference is the passage of time, but I had a feeling that wouldn't go over well. So instead, we simply sat with her, murmuring words of consolation.

"If only we had arrived sooner," she said. "Maybe we could have saved him."

"I was here sooner," Dooley pointed out, "but I was all by myself, and also, Professor Moriarty is a very cunning and dangerous opponent, so I don't think I would have been a match for him." He shivered. "Good thing he didn't see me, or else he might have killed me, too."

"I don't think Professor Moriarty bothers with cats," Brutus pointed out. "He probably goes after the big-ticket items. Like this Holmes person you keep mentioning."

We all glanced at him. "You don't know who Sherlock Holmes is?" I asked, unable to keep the incredulity from my voice.

"No, I don't think I've had the pleasure," said Brutus. "He looked like a funny old bird, though. Living in a house that's so decayed on the outside and so clean on the inside. Though someone told me once that people do it on purpose, you know. Make it look as if they're dirt poor so burglars won't take an interest. Though this Moriarty feller clearly wasn't fooled. You have to tell Odelia, Dooley. So she and Chase can arrest the guy. It isn't often that a murder is solved almost before it's been committed, so I guess that's a stroke of luck for the good guys."

"But sweetie pie," said Harriet. "Sherlock Holmes doesn't really exist."

"He sure doesn't," said Brutus with a chuckle. "I'm no expert, but I'd say he's definitely passed beyond the veil."

"No, but Sherlock Holmes is a fictional character," Harriet insisted. "And so is Professor Moriarty."

"What do you mean?" asked Brutus, who now looked stricken, as if someone had pulled a dirty trick on him and was trying to make him look like a fool.

"He's a character in a series of novels," I explained. "Written over a hundred years ago. He's a fictional detective, like there are many in literature, only he's more famous and more popular than most and has really put his stamp on the genre of detective fiction. In the books, his opponent was often Professor Moriarty, who is also a fictional character and not a real person."

"Though they could both be based on real people, of course," said Harriet when she saw that her boyfriend was taking this piece of news very hard.

"But... but..." he sputtered. He slowly turned his head to take in Dooley. "But you said..."

"I think the one question we should ask ourselves," said Dooley, who had clearly been following his own line of thought, "is where Doctor Watson is. And Mrs. Hudson, of course. When I was here before, I could have sworn there were other people in the house, which makes me wonder why they didn't do anything to stop Moriarty from murdering his arch-nemesis Sherlock Holmes." He tapped his nose intelligently. "Something is very fishy here, Max. Very fishy indeed."

"The only thing that's fishy is that you're playing me for a fool!" said Brutus.

Dooley looked up with a smile. "Hmm?"

"You told me—"

"Let's not get upset about this," Harriet suggested quickly. "Dooley did what he felt was necessary."

"And I still haven't been able to get my paws on one of Mr. Holmes's pipes," said Dooley.

"I don't need a pipe, Dooley," I told him. "For one thing, I don't smoke, and for another, I'm sure that the last thing we should concern ourselves with right now is pipes."

"Yes, I guess you're right," said Dooley. "But Harriet said she has the greatest gift for your birthday, and also Brutus. So I figured I'd better have an extra-great gift, since I am your best friend, after all. And best friends give each other the best gifts."

"You don't have to give me anything, Dooley," I said. "In fact, I'd much rather not be reminded of my birthday at all."

"But why?" said Harriet, greatly surprised by this. "Don't you like to be pampered and spoiled rotten on your very special day?"

"I most certainly do not," I said.

It was obvious that she couldn't understand this point of view. But then Harriet would enjoy celebrating her birthday every day if it involved being pampered, spoiled, and becoming the center of attention all day long.

"Well, that's too bad," said Harriet. "Cause the gift me and Brutus got you is a day at the pet salon. I spent all day yesterday there myself. For research purposes, of course. Which is why I was asking you about my coat." She preened a little. "They've got this great new shampoo which I think you will simply love! It smells like daffodils and—"

"Look, we better start hunting for clues," I said, "to determine what exactly happened here this morning. So what can you tell us about this man, Dooley?"

"Well, he was wearing a mask," said Dooley slowly as he threw his mind back. "And he was a very powerful man, a little bit like Chase is, you know. Strong and muscular and tall and... well, I don't know if he's handsome like Chase, of course, because of the mask and all that. But I like to think that he was."

"I still can't believe that you fooled me like that," said Brutus, shaking his head. "So there is no Professor Moriarty and no Sherlock Holmes?"

"Only in the world of literature and fiction," I told him with a smile.

"It's fine, sweetie," said Harriet as she gave him a pat on the back. "I hadn't heard of him until very recently either." She gave me a hurt look. "I can't believe you don't like our gift to you, Max. After all the trouble I went to by personally inspecting the place and making sure it was up to our usual standards."

"I'm not big on pet salons, Harriet," I told her. Last time I'd gone to the place they had subjected me to something called anal gland expression and I still hadn't fully recovered from the ordeal, so going back there was the last thing I wanted.

"It's just so horrible!" said Fifi, once again bursting into speech. "A dead body! On my watch! And look at Kurt. He's obviously very shaken as well."

"I think you did a very brave thing, Fifi," I said. "We only had to say the word that someone was being attacked, and immediately you jumped in and vowed to save their life. I think that shows a lot of courage."

"I didn't think. You said a man was being attacked and I simply reacted. It must be some kind of basic instinct that made me jump through that window and go in. Though if I'd known then what I know now, maybe I wouldn't have done it."

"And I think you would. Because you're that kind of dog," I told her.

The smile that slid up her furry features showed that my words had gone a long way to restoring some of her equanimity. "Gee, thanks, Max. That's probably the nicest thing anyone has ever said to me. Maybe we should do this more often."

"No, thanks," said Brutus. "Finding dead bodies might be fine for some, but the less it happens to me, the better."

"Yeah, I guess you're right," said Fifi. "Though it's probably true that you get used to it after a while. Just look at that guy. He seems almost happy this happened."

She was pointing to Abe Cornwall, who had just come walking out of the house, and who did indeed wear a big smile on his face.

"That's the county coroner," I said. "If anyone is used to dealing with dead bodies, it's him. It's his job, after all."

We all watched as he walked up to Chase and Odelia, who had just arrived, and stood conferring with them for a moment. I think the conclusion was pretty straightforward: whoever the man inside that house was, he was definitely dead.

CHAPTER 7

Chase scratched his scalp, and frankly, Odelia felt like doing the same thing. It had been a busy day for both of them already, and it almost seemed as if they had to put out fires all over town. Wilbur Vickery had called the station claiming to have some very important information that he wanted to share. That vital information turned out to be an imminent abduction attempt that would be made on Charlene Butterwick, Odelia's aunt, and an assassination attempt on her uncle Alec. The likely culprit behind these was Charlene's ex-husband, which was impossible, since the man had died of a heart attack a couple of years ago. Clearly, Wilbur had been fed some bad information by whoever his source was.

Next was a young girl who had been found on the street in front of their own home and who was the victim of a hit-and-run accident. She was a twelve-year-old girl who lived further down the street and had been riding her bicycle when she was hit by a speeding van that failed to stop and check if the girl was all right.

And now this. According to Dooley, he had actually

witnessed the attack on the victim and had gone in search of help. But by the time he arrived with his friends in tow, along with Odelia's neighbor Kurt Mayfield, the victim was already dead.

"Heart attack, most likely," Abe Cornwall now said with a touch of disappointment. "I wish I could say he was stabbed, garroted, poisoned or shot, but it is what it is. His heart simply gave up, possibly as a consequence of the stressful circumstances he was being subjected to, if this story you told me about a home invasion is true. I'll be able to tell you more once I get him on my slab. I knew him, you know, Alan Gerard. A regular eccentric. Used to sell encyclopedias from door to door, back when that was still the done thing. But then, of course, encyclopedias went out of fashion, and he lost his job. I met him from time to time at medical conventions and suchlike but hadn't seen him these last couple of years. I'd heard he had become something of a recluse."

"He was a doctor?" asked Odelia.

"Used to be. Brilliant brain surgeon. But then he lost a patient on the operating table and later lost a medical malpractice lawsuit filed against him by the patient's husband, so he was forced to leave the profession, which is when he started peddling encyclopedias. I bought several, and so did many of his colleagues, feeling bad for the poor fellow. But in the end, he became more known for his drinking habit than his stimulating conversation, so he disappeared from the social scene. But to end up like this, the victim of a home invasion—that's just sad. Oh, well. Such is life, I guess." He gave Chase a pat on the back. "Expect my report first thing, detective. And now if you'll excuse me, I've got another stiff to inspect. Accidentally locked himself into a meat locker, of all places. They will keep you on your toes," he added with a chuckle. "Never a dull moment!"

"Now why would anyone attack a man who had lost

everything and was living like a recluse in his own home?" asked Chase. "That makes no sense."

"According to Dooley, he had Mr. Gerard strapped to a chair with a hood pulled over his head and was demanding he tell him where he had stashed the painting. Maybe his attacker thought he had a valuable painting somewhere?"

"It's possible," Chase allowed. "Though if what Abe told us is true, whoever attacked him was barking up the wrong tree. I mean, have you seen the state his house is in?"

They both looked up at the facade, which looked more like one of those ghost mansions you often see in movies. Clearly, Alan Gerard had fallen on hard times and didn't have the money to keep up with repairs on the old place.

"It looks a lot better inside, though," she said.

"Yeah, but old," said Chase. "Once upon a time, this must have been a beautiful house, but now? Not so much anymore. Which makes me wonder why anyone would target that old man, especially if his life story was so well-known."

Chase had tasked his officers to do a house-to-house along the street and see if any of Mr. Gerard's neighbors had seen something, and he had high hopes it would yield a result. And if that was the case, this would be a quick case to solve.

"How did Dooley happen to come upon a home invasion in progress?" asked Chase.

Odelia smiled. "He thought that Sherlock Holmes lived here, and he wanted to give Max an original present, so he figured that if he asked Mr. Holmes if he could have one of his pipes, he would give it to Max, since they're both great detectives."

"Cute," said Chase with a grin.

"The strange thing is that he thought he heard other people in the house," said Odelia. "So it's possible that there was more than one attacker."

"Yeah, that's mostly their MO," said Chase. "One of them tries to get the homeowner to reveal the location of the safe or the valuables, while the other searches the place. Which means we're most likely looking at a gang here."

They watched as the body of the victim was carried out of the house and put into a waiting ambulance. "How old was he?" asked Odelia.

"Seventy-eight." Chase's face worked. "Don't worry, babe. We'll get the animals that did this, and we'll make sure they go away for a very long time."

CHAPTER 8

Dooley hadn't really paid attention to what Max and his friends had been talking about. It was a terrible shame that poor Mr. Sherlock had died, of course, but on the other hand—now that he was dead, he wouldn't be needing his pipes anymore, would he? And since Max was still very much alive, he needed those pipes a lot more. And so while the others discussed the ins and outs of what they called a home invasion gone wrong, Dooley decided to take a peek inside the house and look for those pipes.

Max had said he didn't need a present, and that he didn't even like to be reminded that he had a birthday coming up, but Dooley didn't really believe that. Everyone likes to be celebrated, and that included Max, and so he knew for sure that if he gave Max a present like that, his friend would be over the moon.

The house was still teeming with police officers, who were searching high and low for the attackers of that poor detective. Dooley could have told them that they were wasting their time, since the attackers had left a long time ago. But then humans are often a little slower to get wise to things than cats. And so, as he snuck between the legs of a cop who came trotting down the stairs with a box in his hands, no doubt eager to show it to Chase, who was in charge of the investigation, he stealthily made his way upstairs and soon found himself in what looked like the study of the great detective.

Contrary to what he had expected, he didn't see any sign of the long and successful career Mr. Holmes had enjoyed. No framed letters of gratitude from satisfied clients. No mementos from any of his famous cases: no lock of hair of the Baskerville dog, no scarf belonging to Irene Adler, no teeth of the Sussex vampire. In fact, all he found were medical diplomas and thick, dusty medical tomes occupying the bookshelves. He even saw several encyclopedias, but nothing that referred to the detective trade.

And then he understood. Clearly, Mr. Holmes had been a very modest man and didn't like to brag. He almost became emotional as he thought about what kind of person Mr. Holmes must have been: brilliant but humble. What a guy.

He jumped up onto the man's desk in search of his collection of meerschaum pipes, and when he couldn't find them, wondered if maybe he'd stored them in a different room. Or maybe he'd tucked them into one of his desk drawers? Oddly enough, he couldn't even sniff a whiff of pipe or tobacco anywhere in the room.

And then the awful truth finally dawned on him. Oh, no!

In his later years, Mr. Holmes must have quit smoking!

It was often that way. Happily sucking on a pipe when they were young, or smoking a cigarette, and then once they reached middle age, they figured that the habit didn't agree with them as much as it used to, and so they quit.

How awful. How disappointing!

And as he was about to hop back down from the great detective's desk, he saw a piece of paper with a few notes jotted down on it. Curious, he started reading the note, wondering if it was a clue to one of the man's mysteries.

As far as he could tell, the note referred to 'the case of the missing second sock,' and it wasn't as fascinating or riveting as many of the man's other cases had been. The gist of it was that a box of socks had arrived and one of the packages had contained only a single sock instead of the usual pair. It also contained the rough draft of a rambling but strongly-worded complaint directed at the sock company.

Odd, Dooley felt. It didn't really feel like a life-or-death case. Then again, it proved to him what a great man the dearly departed detective had been, if even a minor case like this had obviously commanded his full attention.

He sighed and sincerely hoped that Chase and Odelia would catch the culprit, with the assistance of Max, of course. Though without a pipe, he wasn't sure if Max's mind would work on all cylinders as usual.

He jumped down to the floor again and saw a cigarette butt lying behind the curtain. And since it was better than nothing, he carefully picked it up between his teeth and hurried out of the room with it.

It wasn't a pipe, of course, but it pretty much amounted to the same thing.

Once outside, he deposited the cigarette in front of his friend, a proud smile creasing his features. "Happy birthday, Max! I know it's not a pipe, but this cigarette belonged to the great detective Sherlock Holmes."

Brutus gave it a look of distaste. "And what is Max supposed to do with an old cigarette butt? Smoke it?"

"No, you can draw inspiration from it," Dooley suggested. "Knowing that at one time it was being smoked by a mind almost as great as yours."

"Why... thank you, Dooley," said Max, who was so overcome with emotion that he didn't know quite how to react.

How endearing. And so Dooley, glowing with pride, cast a look at Harriet, as if to say: now top that, if you can!

"Where did you find this?" asked Harriet, studying the butt closely.

"It was lying behind the curtain in Sherlock's study," said Dooley. He would have confessed that he had gone there to borrow a pipe from the man's collection, but he felt that this information would lead them away from appreciating the real treasure he had brought. "Between the curtain and the window."

"What is it, sweetie?" asked Brutus.

"Well, Sherlock was an old man, right?"

"He was," Max confirmed. "Though his name wasn't Sherlock but Alan Gerard. He was seventy-eight."

"See that lipstick? Either Mr. Gerard liked to wear lipstick, or this cigarette was smoked by a woman."

Dooley's face fell. Oh, of all the rotten luck! Now he'd gone and found Max the perfect present, and it turned out to belong to Mrs. Hudson instead of Mr. Holmes!

CHAPTER 9

Sonny Hayworth had arrived home with his modest treasure, but when he cooked his daughter the perfect feast to end all feasts, she didn't seem particularly pleased or even hungry.

"I already ate," she said, pushing her plate away, much to Sonny's distress.

"Hey, do you know what I had to do to put this most excellent meal on the table?" he demanded.

Kiki shrugged. As usual, she was engrossed in her cell phone, probably texting with her friends from school, or maybe her boyfriend. Even though she was only fifteen, she claimed to have a boyfriend already, which couldn't be right. But since she only spent every other weekend with her dad, it wasn't as if he had a lot of control over what she did or didn't do when his ex-wife had her. He'd already told Val that she should keep a closer eye on their daughter, but clearly she didn't care.

"Just have a taste," he said. "It's pretty yummy."

"Oh, Dad," she said with an eye roll.

"Just a little taste. You know you want to. Your dad's pasta is the best in the universe, remember?"

That line may have worked when she was seven, but it obviously didn't make a big impression now. Instead, she held out her hand. "Can I have my allowance now, please?"

His mood sank. "Your allowance? Is it that time of the month already?"

"Yes, it is, Dad." But when he didn't budge, she sighed deeply. "You ran out of money again, is that it?"

It was extremely embarrassing for any dad to have to admit to his daughter that he is poor, and so he searched around for an excuse to explain the delay in her monthly allowance. "You know what? A friend of mine is in the hospital, so I've been helping him out. And you know that hospitals are expensive, don't you? Remember when your grandpa Joe was in the hospital and we had to organize that fundraiser?"

"Maybe you should organize a fundraiser for yourself, Dad," she said as she got up from the table.

"Hey, where are you going?"

"I've got a date with my boyfriend," she said. "He's picking me up on his motorcycle."

"Motorcycle? How old is this kid?!"

"Sixteen. Bye, Dad. And please get me my allowance next time, will you? Then I won't have to tell Mom."

There were so many things he wanted to say to that, that by the time the door slammed he still hadn't said a word. Instead, he just sat there feeling pretty miserable. Then he looked down at his plate, and his daughter's plate, and a sudden righteous anger welled up in him. It was all that stupid cat's fault. If it hadn't squealed on him, he wouldn't have told that shopkeeper about that business with the mayor. And if he hadn't told him about the mayor, he might still have been able to get in on the deal, since they'd offered him the job of babysitter.

If only he'd said yes, then he would have been able to pay his bills and give Kiki her allowance. But now that the cops knew, of course the deal was off.

And it was all because of that stupid cat!

* * *

KINGMAN WAS ON A ROLL. Since there wasn't a lot more we could do at the house belonging to that poor Mr. Gerard, we decided to take a stroll into town. The neighborhood canvass Chase had ordered hadn't revealed a lot, except one neighbor had seen a white van race away from the scene at a high rate of speed with two men inside. Unfortunately, he hadn't gotten a good look at the men, and the license plate was a mystery to him as well. But at least it was something, and Odelia thought it might be connected to the girl who had been hit by a van while riding her bicycle on Harrington Street. And if that was the case, they might be able to get more witness statements.

And since the police force was out in full force to track down the miscreants who had caused Mr. Gerard's death, it was clear that our assistance in the matter was no longer required. We had delivered the cigarette butt to Odelia, who had handed it over to Chase, who said it probably belonged to one of Mr. Gerard's guests or maybe a cleaning lady, and didn't seem to think a lot of it. Nevertheless, he had still tucked it away in one of those little plastic evidence bags he likes to carry around with him, and that seemed to satisfy everyone involved that everything was being done to bring this sordid business to a conclusion.

"You should have seen the look on his face," Kingman

now told us in an animated fashion. "Scared to death he was! Caught! By a cat, no less!"

"How did you find out he was stealing?" asked Brutus, who loved listening to these stories of heroics.

"Well, I saw him, didn't I? Saw him with my own two eyes. He had on one of those long coats with many pockets, and when he took it off, out came all of this stuff! Cheese and tomato sauce and spaghetti—and not the cheapest brands either. This guy had taste. Only the best would do. And since Wilbur was chatting up some lady customer, I decided I wasn't going to let him get away with this. So I started screaming my head off, and that stopped him right in his tracks."

"But how did Wilbur know you were trying to stop a thief?" asked Harriet.

"Because he knew the guy. Turns out he'd caught him before doing the same thing. And now that he was up to his old tricks again, Wilbur was really upset, cause the last time the guy had promised it wouldn't happen again."

I have to say I wasn't all that interested in the tale of a shoplifter being caught, since I figured this probably happens all the time in shops all over the country. But since Kingman was happy that he played the hero, and was reveling in the attention his feat of derring-do brought him, I politely listened and murmured in the right places and awarded him all the laurels his heroics had earned him.

"I almost caught a murderer," said Dooley. "But before I could stop him, it was too late, and Sherlock Holmes was already dead."

For a moment, Kingman was a little confused. "Sherlock Holmes? What are you talking about?" Clearly, he didn't enjoy that someone interrupted his story, even though at this point he had already told us his tale about five times, and I was pretty sure he would go on to tell us about a dozen times more if not checked.

"Professor Moriarty murdered Sherlock Holmes because he wouldn't give up his collection of pipes, and I could have saved him if only I'd moved a little faster." He gave us a sad look. "But it was not to be."

"How do you know that these home invaders were after the guy's pipe collection?" asked Brutus.

"Well, isn't it obvious? I looked for the pipes and they weren't there, which means they must have been stolen."

It was certainly a piece of logic that couldn't be argued with.

"But you said they were after some painting," Harriet pointed out.

"Probably a painting of the pipes," Dooley said, nodding intelligently.

"I still don't get it," said Kingman. "Is there a guy called Sherlock Holmes living in town?"

"His actual name is Alan Gerard," I said, "but Dooley likes to refer to him as Sherlock Holmes."

"I'm sure Alan Gerard is an alias," our friend now claimed. "Because Sherlock Holmes was retired, and he didn't want his mortal enemy Professor Moriarty to find out where he lived. But he did, since Professor Moriarty is a criminal mastermind, and so he found his arch-nemesis and murdered him in cold blood."

Kingman directed a quizzical look at me, and I shook my head once. Kingman got the message and raised his eyebrows. "Ah, well. Looks like it's been one of those days again. I caught a shoplifter, Dooley almost caught a killer, and tonight I'm going to stop Shanille from making the biggest mistake of her life." After that statement, he gave us a shrewd look, knowing full well that he now had our undivided attention.

"What mistake?" said Harriet.

"Shanille is going on a trip. Well, not by herself, obviously. Father Reilly is going to Rome, and she is going to tag along."

We all shared a look of surprise. "Shanille is going to Rome?" asked Brutus.

"That's right. She's going to meet the Pope and get his blessing. Or at least that's what she thinks. Personally, I don't think Father Reilly would be dumb enough to drag his cat halfway around the world and then plunk her on Saint Peter's Square in front of His Holiness the Pope. Vatican security will probably take one look at him and tell him to get rid of the cat before he can come anywhere close to Papa. They're not going to risk the guy getting foot-and-mouth disease."

"Pretty sure that only applies to cows and pigs and such," I told our friend. "Not cats, since we don't have hooves."

"Whatever," said Kingman, satisfied that his stunning revelation had put him in the center of attention again. "Pretty sure Francis is going to drop her off at one of those pet hotels and pick her up again once he's back from his trip."

"But she can stay with us," said Dooley, much to Harriet's consternation.

"No way!" said the Persian. "Are you nuts? Imagine having to share our home with that cat. She'll probably boss us around from the moment she arrives till the moment she leaves. No, I'm definitely putting my paw down on this one."

"What are you guys talking about?" suddenly a familiar voice sounded from behind us.

When we turned around, we found we had been joined by the choir conductor herself.

CHAPTER 10

"*I* was just talking about your trip to Rome," said Kingman blithely. "And how much you're looking forward to it."

Shanille deigned a tiny smirk. "It's going to be absolutely heavenly," she announced. "We're going to meet the Pope and we're going to be blessed by that great man himself, and we're going to take plenty of pictures. We might even get a private audience with His Holiness, and it wouldn't surprise me if he announced that Father Reilly will be moving up a few steps in the world."

"Steps up? What steps up?" asked Brutus, who isn't as well-versed in Catholic lore as Shanille. But then I guess none of us are.

"I think the reason Father Reilly is being called to Rome is because His Holiness has seen what a great and beloved leader he is to his flock, and that his shoulders are strong enough and his faith mature enough to accept a higher calling."

"Huh?" said Kingman, very eloquently, I thought.

"Bishop, Kingman," said Shanille with a slight diminution

of her understated exuberance. "Or maybe even cardinal." She smiled a beatific smile even as she directed her eyes heavenward, as if to thank the good Lord personally for this great honor. "Cardinal Reilly. It does have a nice ring to it, don't you think? And then maybe one day... His Holiness? Imagine me, a papal cat. Wouldn't that be something?"

"But wouldn't you have to move to Rome if that happened?" asked Kingman.

"Of course I would have to move to Rome, Kingman," she snapped. "Or do you really think the entire Vatican will move to Hampton Cove?"

"But then you wouldn't be able to lead cat choir anymore!" said Dooley, as the meaning of Shanille's words penetrated his mind, such as it is.

"It's a sacrifice I'm willing to make," she said haughtily. "And who knows? I might be leading the Sistine Chapel Choir next."

I'd never heard of this Sistine Chapel choir before, so I asked, inadvisably perhaps, "Does the Vatican have a choir that consists of cats, too?"

She shot me a look that reeked of fire and brimstone. "Don't be silly, Max. Of course there is no Vatican cat choir. I mean the actual Sistine Chapel Choir, that consists of boys with the most angelic voices you've ever heard. To lead that choir would be the fulfillment of my life's dream. The crowning glory of my work."

"But... you're a cat," I said. "How can you lead a human choir?"

She sighed and shook her head, as if I'd asked the silliest question. "Oh, Max. Where is your faith? Where is your trust in the Lord's ways?"

I knew the Lord worked in mysterious ways his wonders to perform, but I'd never heard that he gave a cat the power to conduct a choir of actual people. But since I didn't want to stir up trouble or get locked in some kind of argument, I merely smiled and nodded. "It sounds like a great opportunity, Shanille."

"Please call me Philomena from now on."

"Philomena?"

"I'm trying on the name for size, anticipating the day I move to Rome."

We all goggled at her for a moment, but she took it in stride.

"But you're absolutely right, Max, it is a wonderful opportunity. In fact, the greatest opportunity there is. I just hope I'm worthy." She bowed her head for a moment in benign humility, then looked up again, beaming. "But don't worry. I'll never forget you guys. After all, you gave me the chance to hone my craft. To become a better choir leader—a better leader in general—and a better cat. So I bid you adieu for now, and if you're ever in Rome, make an appointment with my secretary, and I'll see if I can slot you into my no doubt very busy schedule." And with these words, she turned on her heel and strode off.

For a moment, none of us spoke, then Harriet scoffed, "What a load of—"

"Now, Harriet," said Kingman with a twinkle in his eye. "Be careful what you say. You don't want the leader of the Sistine Chapel Choir to accuse you of blasphemy."

"No way is she coming to stay with us," said Harriet. "She can go to her cat hotel and be happy about it. I mean, I knew she was arrogant, but this?"

"She does seem very sure that she will get this position," I said. "And also about Father Reilly's promotion."

"Do they call it a promotion?" asked Brutus. "When a priest becomes a bishop? And then a cardinal and then the Pope?"

"I guess so," I said. Though, like I said, I'm not well-versed either in Catholic lore or the lingo. Then again, it seemed a bit of a stretch to assume that Father Reilly had been called to Rome because the Pope wanted to handle his succession. That much I knew about the Vatican, that it didn't exactly work like that.

"But if Shanille is going to Rome," said Dooley, "then who is going to lead cat choir?"

All eyes turned to Harriet, who gave us a coy look. "Now you guys, that's very kind of you and all, and I'm sure I feel honored by the privilege, but I'm not sure I've got the chops. After all, those are some big shoes to fill—so to speak."

"I wouldn't worry about it if I were you," said Brutus. "Shanille isn't going to Rome, and Father Reilly isn't going to be the next Pope, so she'll stay right here and continue to run the cat choir."

"I'm not so sure," I said. Somehow I had a feeling that things were about to change in Hampton Cove. Call it a premonition, but as we watched Shanille sashay off along the street, blessing cats left and right by waving her paw, I wasn't sure if she'd even want to run cat choir. Clearly, she had left all of that behind, determined as she was to follow along on the path to a bright and glorious future as a papal cat.

CHAPTER 11

"You shouldn't have hit that guy, Johnny."
"But I didn't hit him! I only threatened him a little."
"So then why did he suddenly keel over and die, huh? Tell me that!"
"Because he was old? Old people sometimes just die on you, Jer."
"I still think you hit him, and that's why he went and died."

Ever since that disaster at Alan Gerard's place, Jerry had been accusing Johnny of being to blame for what happened to that poor old guy, and try as he might, he couldn't convince his partner that it had nothing to do with him.

"Poor guy just went and died on me," he repeated. "Like a chicken. Just keeled over and croaked. And he hadn't even told me what I wanted to know."

That was the worst part of the whole deal. They'd gone over that place from top to bottom, but hadn't found anything worth taking. Not like the small fortune they'd been promised they'd find on the premises. And then of course, after the guy breathed his last, they figured they'd better skedaddle before someone pinned it on them. Their parole officer wouldn't be happy. The last time they'd been arrested was when they were selling vitamins to kids—though as it later turned out it wasn't vitamins but amphetamines, which apparently was illegal—and now murder? They'd probably lock them up and throw away the key!

They sat in the unmarked white van they liked to drive these days and contemplated their next course of action. That was the disadvantage of their line of business: even though sometimes you hit it big, other times you struck out. Not like you if worked for the DMV and collected a regular paycheck.

On the sidewalk, a seething mass of people strode past, on their way to wherever they were going. It set the seal on Johnny's sense of doom.

"Maybe we should get a nine-to-five job, just like all of those other bozos out there," he said moodily. "It's probably a lot easier than being small-time contractors like we are."

"Small-time contractors are in line to one day become big-time contractors," said Jerry, who was picking something from his teeth with his fingernail. "Whereas those poor schmucks will never amount to anything. All they can do is wait for retirement, and then be surprised when their 401(k) ends up going bust because someone had his hand in the cookie jar and they get nothing."

"But we got nothing, Jer," he reminded his partner.

"Just you wait and see. One of these days we're going to strike it big, Johnny. I can feel it in my gut. There. That's her."

He pointed to Charlene Butterwick, mayor of Hampton Cove, who had exited Town Hall and now stood talking to some other folks on the steps. She was holding a stack of files in one hand and a briefcase in the other and looked more like a lawyer than a small-town mayor, Johnny thought.

"Are you sure about this, Jer?" he asked. Maybe Jerry felt in his gut that they were about to strike big, but what he felt in his gut was quite the opposite.

"Sure I'm sure. Got your balaclava?"

"Uh-huh," he said as he grabbed his balaclava and pulled it over his head.

"Got your piece?"

"Sure thing, Jer," he said as he fingered his handgun.

"Then let's do this. Remember, you grab her and pull her into the van while I make sure no one gets any funny ideas about getting in our way. Got it?"

He sighed. "If you're sure about this."

Jerry looked over with a curious look on his face. "You really are in a funk, aren't you? This ain't like you, Johnny."

"It's the dead guy," he admitted.

"Forget about the dead guy! Like you said, he was going to die anyway. Just our rotten luck, that's all."

"If you say so, Jer."

"Here she comes. Look alive."

He glanced in the side mirror and saw that Mayor Butterwick was alone and heading in their direction. And since he figured that Jerry probably knew best, as he was the brains of the outfit and Johnny was the brawn, he swiftly stepped out of the van and pulled his gun on the woman. "No funny business!" he yelled.

And before the woman could recover from the shock of coming face to face with a gangster with a gun pointing directly at her, she stuck up her hands.

"Don't shoot!" she yelled, which Johnny thought was funny, since he didn't have any intention to shoot. In fact, his gun wasn't even loaded.

While Jerry scanned the perimeter for anyone foolish enough to intervene, Johnny yanked open the side door of the van and assisted the mayor into the vehicle, then slammed the door shut again.

Jerry hopped behind the wheel, and moments later, they were peeling away from the sidewalk.

The whole operation had lasted about ten seconds—maybe even less.

"What do you want?" Mayor Butterwick shouted from the rear.

"That went pretty well," said Jerry with satisfaction.

"Yeah, I thought so," Johnny agreed. At least the woman hadn't died on them. Then he remembered something. "Shouldn't we, you know, sedate her?"

Jerry thunked his forehead. "I knew I'd forgotten something!"

Well, it was too late now.

"Hey—let me out of here!" Mayor Butterwick shouted and pounded the metal divider. "Let me out of here right now! My husband is the chief of police, and he will not be happy, I can tell you that right now!"

Oh, boy. This was gonna be a long day.

CHAPTER 12

Kingman watched as his friends took their leave. He shook his head and chuckled when he thought of Shanille and her aspirations to become a papal cat. Of all the crazy things... As the cat belonging to Wilbur Vickery, he had always been located right at the heart of Main Street, and as a consequence, he was probably the most sought-after cat in all of Hampton Cove. He knew everybody, and everybody knew him. And since cats love to talk, and Kingman even more so than most, there wasn't a single snippet of news that happened that he wasn't aware of. In a sense, he was like the local paper for cats, and so it wouldn't be long before he had told and retold the news about Shanille's papal ambitions to all and sundry. Before the day was through, there wouldn't be a single cat in town who wouldn't know about the conductor's move to Vatican City —if it ever happened.

He got down from his throne—one of the crates Wilbur liked to pack tomatoes in, but with a nice blanket draped on top and some old copies of the *Hampton Cove Gazette* for extra padding—and made his way inside. All this talking had made him thirsty, and so he padded to the back of the store, through the screen curtain and into the private space that he shared with Wilbur. And he had just settled down to enjoy a few nuggets of kibble and a sip of water when he became aware of a man standing at the door that led to the small backyard. He recognized the man as Sonny Hayworth, who had tried to rob all of that stuff earlier.

And if he wasn't mistaken, the man had bad business on his mind.

The door opened, and Kingman still sat frozen, staring at the crook.

"Here, kitty, kitty," said the guy as he reached out a tentative hand.

The last thing Kingman was going to do was to come 'here,' or wherever else this guy wanted to take him. And so with his typically languid response, he held up one paw and then dug his claws deeply into the man's outstretched hand.

Sonny yelped in surprise and agony, and as he retracted his injured hand, directed a look at Kingman of such hatred that Kingman wondered if perhaps he'd overdone things. Then again, clearly the guy wasn't there to give him a nice pat on the head and thank him for his service. At least if the burlap sack he was holding in his other hand was any indication.

"Now buzz off, bozo," he said as he gave his paw a lick.

At that moment, Wilbur came running. "What's with all the racket?!" he demanded heatedly. For a moment, he stood face to face with Sonny. "You!" he said. Then he directed a look at the man's bleeding hand, the sack, and put two and two together in a heartbeat. "You were trying to steal my cat!" he cried.

"No, I wasn't," said Sonny.

"Yes, you were!"

"I swear to God I wasn't!"

For a moment, the two men stood squaring off, then finally Sonny shrugged. "My daughter likes cats. So I figured I'd take your cat's picture and show it to her. After all, he is by far the most handsome cat in all of Hampton Cove."

"Oh, will you clear off already?" said Wilbur, who wasn't buying any of this.

"Will do," said Sonny and quickly did as he was told.

Wilbur crouched down next to Kingman and inspected his paw. "Are you all right, buddy? Did that bad man hurt you?"

"No, he didn't," he assured his human. "I hurt him a little, though."

"Oh, my precious baby," said Wilbur, who, as a man who didn't have kids, loved his cat like other people would love their offspring—or maybe even more.

"Look, it's fine," said Kingman. "But if he comes back, I can tell you right now I won't be held responsible for the consequences. I may even use my other paw."

Wilbur stared at the door as he idly massaged Kingman's neck. "I wonder what he was up to. Do you think this is because you gave him away earlier?"

"Revenge, you mean? Wouldn't surprise me one bit," Kingman said.

"Maybe you better stay close to me today," Wilbur suggested. "If he tried once, he may try again. Though next time I lay eyes on that guy, I'm calling the cops."

"Better call Vesta," Kingman suggested. "She'll make short shrift of the guy."

"Or maybe I should tell Vesta. For some reason, and I don't know why, most people are more afraid of her than they are of the cops."

"That's because she's fierce and takes no nonsense."

"I'll move your bowls to the front of the store for now,"

Wilbur suggested as he picked up Kingman's bowls. "No opportunity, no thief, you know."

And since he had operated one of the most popular stores in town for decades now, Wilbur knew a thing or two about thieves—and now also about catnappers!

And they'd just returned to the front of the store when a white van passed by on the street. And as Kingman happened to glance at the driver, he thought he recognized that other incorrigible crook, Johnny Carew.

He shook his head as he remembered how Johnny and his partner in crime, Jerry Vale, had once kidnapped all of Hampton Cove's cats. It made him wonder if he shouldn't get himself a bodyguard. Which is when he suddenly got a bright idea.

CHAPTER 13

"Waiter. Waiter! There's a hair in my soup!"

"I'm so sorry, sir. I'll get you a new plate immediately."

"It's a very big hair," said the customer, who looked extremely irate. "And very dark." He darted a suspicious look at the waiter's head, but when he saw that the waiter was bald, his gaze softened. "Must be from the chef," he announced.

Roger Turton, who had just stepped out of the kitchen to take a look around the restaurant, overheard the conversation, and his heart stopped. The last thing a chef wants to hear is that a customer has found an ingredient in his dish that has no business whatsoever being there. Like a hair or a nail or a used band-aid. Since his own hair was blond, this particular hair couldn't possibly belong to him, but of course, that was no consolation.

Other customers had picked up on the conversation since the customer had made no effort to lower his voice or be discreet about his discovery. Not unlike Indiana Jones hitting upon some gold idol or precious medallion, he seemed almost pleased with his discovery and wanted the whole world to know about it, or at least the rest of the Hungry Pipe's diners.

Roger saw it all happening with a rising sense of panic. He saw phones come out and people starting to capture the scene on video. He saw other customers subject their own dishes to a closer scrutiny, eager to make a similar discovery.

God, this was a nightmare. And the waiter's behavior didn't help. Seeming almost to relish in the sudden attention he had garnered, he was carrying that plate to the kitchen as if holding a dead rat in front of him, his face screwed up in distaste and doing a slow walk to the kitchen, making sure those filming him got their money's worth.

"Hurry up, you fool!" he hissed the moment the man was within earshot. "Move it, move it, move it!"

When the man finally caught sight of the big boss, he finally put some pep in his step and covered the final couple of yards in record time, and they both disappeared into the kitchen, where mercifully they were out of earshot and out of view from the now practically baying crowd.

"A hair in the soup, chef," he said. He pointed to the hair in question. "Big and long and black. Can't be mine, chef."

"No, I can see that," he grumbled. He took over the plate and subjected the hair to a closer scrutiny. He could almost have sworn… He darted a suspicious look at his sous-chef, who had hair of a lustrous and thick variety. Very dark as well. Could he be the hair's originator? But then he discarded the notion. Marco was a professional and had come highly recommended from the restaurant where he had worked before. And besides, like all the chefs in the kitchen, he wore a cap so nothing like this would happen.

"It could be from the customer himself, chef," the waiter now suggested. "Sometimes they do that, you know. To get a free meal? It's a known trick."

"I know it's a known trick," he said, then instructed the man to take a fresh plate and tell the couple that their meal was on the house.

"But you're only encouraging them to do it again, chef," the waiter lamented. "And inspiring others to do the same. Just you wait and see. They'll all be 'finding' hairs in their soup now."

"Just take it already, will you?" he said, tired of arguing with this kid.

"Oh, all right," said the waiter. "But don't say I didn't warn you."

His wife now returned from her smoke break and gave him a puzzled look.

"A customer found a hair in his soup," he told her. He showed the hair in question.

"It isn't mine," she said immediately. Like him, she was blond, with very fine hair that felt soft to the touch. He would know since it was one of the things that had attracted him to her in the first place. That and her quick-wittedness.

"I know. Ludo thinks it might be the customer trying to get a free meal. And he might be right."

"Do you want me to go and apologize?"

"I already arranged for another plate and told them the meal is on the house."

She studied him for a moment. "You look stressed. Is everything all right?"

"I'm fine," he assured her. "Just one of those days, you know."

She gave him a sweet kiss on the lips and disappeared through the swinging doors. As he glanced over, he caught Marco darting a look in his direction then quickly looking away again. He gave the man a feeble smile to indicate that everything was A-okay and Marco nodded unsmilingly then returned to his work.

That was the problem if you were in charge of the kitchen of a restaurant of the stature of the Hungry Pipe: you had to project self-confidence, calm, and equanimity at all times, and be in full control of your kitchen, or else things could unravel very quickly. And so even though he was feeling frazzled, he made a conscious effort to pull himself together and carry on.

Like he had told Kirsten, it was just one of those days.

CHAPTER 14

We had just arrived home when the news came that Charlene Butterwick had been abducted, in broad daylight, in front of Town Hall! Gran, who told us the astonishing news, immediately told us to drop whatever we were doing and launch a full-scale investigation, enlisting our 'Baker Street Cats' and generally putting our ear to the ground to pick up any hint of who might be responsible for this heinous and most brazen crime.

"How is Uncle Alec?" asked Brutus.

"Going to pieces, what do you think?" said Gran. "Though he's trying to hold it together, for Charlene's sake."

"And they just had their honeymoon," said Dooley, shaking his head as if Charlene was already dead.

"We will find her, Dooley," Gran stressed, "and whoever did this will be sorry."

"I'll bet they're sorry already," said Harriet. "Probably they didn't know that Charlene is the mayor, and married to the chief of police."

"Oh, I'll bet they knew exactly who she was," said Gran. "And that the first ransom demand will come in very soon now." She threw up her hands. "What is the world coming to?" And with these words, she took off to enlist the other members of her neighborhood watch to take this matter firmly in hand and do what they could to bring about the happy ending.

As for us, we decided to head downtown to the scene of the crime and do as Gran had suggested: enlist our vast network of pets to discover who had taken Charlene and where they had taken her.

"This really is a very eventful day, isn't it, Max?" said Dooley as we set about to launch our inquiry. "First that poor Sherlock Holmes being attacked, then the girl on the street being run down, and now Charlene kidnapped. If this keeps up, Hampton Cove will become a hotbed of crime and we'll be in all the papers."

"I very much doubt that will ever be the case, Dooley," I said. "We may be faced with a few incidents today, but in general, Hampton Cove is still a peaceful town."

"I wonder if I should accept the offer or not," said Harriet as the four of us walked along the sidewalk.

"What offer?" asked Brutus.

"Why, the honor of becoming the new conductor of cat choir, of course. If I accept—and I'm not saying I will—I have a few conditions, of course."

We shared a look of astonishment. "Sugar britches, Charlene has been abducted," Brutus said, voicing the general sentiment, "so maybe that should take precedence right now?"

"Oh, but it does—of course it does. Poor Charlene. Poor, poor Charlene. So I think I'll ask for a trailer. All stars have a trailer. And it should be nice and big and comfy. And then I'm also thinking I need a snack. You can't conduct a choir for hours and not take the occasional break. So we should definitely have a craft services table. And I should probably ask for an assistant who can take over and do the difficult bits. I mean, nobody can expect a star of my caliber to be on her paws all the time. So I was thinking I could start things off with a nice little pep talk and then leave the actual conducting to my assistants. That's how it should be done." She gave us a dazzling smile. "Those are my conditions—take it or leave it."

I would have told her to leave it, but then my mind was occupied with other things at that moment. Charlene is Odelia's aunt by marriage, and so an integral part of the family. I just hoped that whoever had taken her wouldn't harm her.

"Poor Charlene," said Dooley now. "She's probably terrified. Scared to death."

I gulped. We had been abducted ourselves, and it wasn't a picnic. In fact, it is one of the more harrowing experiences one can go through. Luckily, in our case, it wasn't long before we managed to free ourselves, but I didn't think Charlene would be in the same position. These people probably had thought things through before they grabbed her off the street. In fact, it sounded to me as if this was the work of a highly professional gang of kidnappers. Experts, in other words, who would make sure that their quarry couldn't possibly get away.

"Yeah, poor Charlene," I echoed. "I just hope they won't hurt her."

"Or I could ask you to be my assistant, sugar lips," Harriet now suggested. "Or even all three of you. You could take turns directing cat choir while I give you instructions from the comfort and safety of my trailer. How does that sound?"

Dooley rolled his eyes. "Oh, Harriet," he said, much to the latter's consternation.

* * *

JOHNNY WAS HURRYING to bring their guest the meal she had requested. It wasn't exactly haute cuisine, but it would have to do for now. The moment they had arrived at their destination—a dilapidated old farmhouse that had been empty for many years—the mayor had demanded to be released. And when they made it clear that wasn't going to happen, she had demanded that she be properly fed.

"I'm hungry," she said as she inspected her new surroundings with a look of distinct distaste. "So unless you want me to starve to death, you're going to have to feed me and feed me well. Is that understood?"

"Yes, Madam Mayor," Johnny had said with the kind of deference and nervousness he always felt when he was in the presence of a figure of authority.

Before they had set about the abduction, they had first made sure the fridge and the freezer were filled to capacity with enough frozen meals to last them at least a couple of weeks. Since they had no idea how long it would be before she was released, they might be stuck with the woman for quite a while.

He unlocked the door and shuffled into the room where they had put up their prisoner. It was the nicest room in the house, but clearly that fact had escaped the mayor, for she now gave Johnny a look of abhorrence. "This place is filthy!" she exclaimed the moment he walked through the door. "It's a disgrace!"

"I'm afraid it's the best we could do on such short notice," he informed her. "But if you would like to lodge a formal complaint, you can always post a review on Yelp." He put the tray on the small ramshackle table near the window. He'd put a tablecloth down to mask the cracks the table had sustained over long years of use and to add a little flourish. It had also been his idea to get a potted plant—the yellow variety—to cheer things up a little and make their guest feel at home. "It's some pretty decent grub," he said proudly as he gestured to the meal. "Prime brand."

"I like freshly cooked food," said Madam Mayor as she took a critical glance at the plate. "These prepared meals all contain too much salt and other chemical additives. They will give you cancer. Do you want me to die of cancer?"

"No, Madam Mayor," he said hastily. "I don't want you to die of anything."

"Food poisoning, maybe?"

"No, Madam Mayor," he admitted as he wrung his hands nervously. For some reason, she suddenly reminded him of his late grandmother, who used to put him over her knee whenever he had been up to something.

"Then cook me something fresh. You can cook, I suppose?"

"Well..." Then he brightened. "Jerry can cook. You wouldn't think so when you saw him, but he really can. He used to cook for Marlene—that's his ex-wife."

"If she's his ex-wife, I don't expect his cooking skills are very good."

"Oh, but they are. I'll tell him to cook you something delicious, and you'll see."

"So your friend is called Jerry. What's your name?"

"Johnny," he said, before belatedly realizing he probably shouldn't have said that. But then the mayor had that effect on him. "I mean, maybe it's not?"

"And I think it is. So Johnny Carew and Jerry Vale, huh? Up to your old tricks again, I see. So who has hired you this time? It can't be Blake Carrington, since he's still in prison. So who is it? And what do they want?"

"I'm not supposed to tell you," he said.

"That's obvious. So who is it? Who hired you to kidnap me?"

"You'd have to ask Jerry," he said truthfully. "He's in

charge of all that." Frankly, he had no idea who had asked Jerry to pick up the mayor. It all seemed a little risky, especially considering that she seemed to know who they were.

"You can take off that mask now, Carew," said the mayor. "We have met before."

And so he took off his mask, which was too small for his face anyway, and didn't obscure as much as it should. "How did you know?" he asked.

She gave him a wintry smile. "Maybe you should quit now and let me go. How about that? And if you do, maybe I'll consider putting in a good word for you with the judge."

His eyes went wide. "You're friends with the judge?"

"Of course. Judge Parker and I go way back. So if you let me make a phone call, I'll make sure he's lenient when he decides on your sentence."

He thought for a moment, then shook his head. "I'm not sure Jerry will like it," he confessed. "He seems very excited about this job. Says it'll net us enough to retire to a non-extradition country."

Charlene sighed. "Oh, Johnny, Johnny. Can't you make up your own mind for once? Do you always have to play second fiddle to that no-good Jerry Vale?"

But since he happened to like Jerry, he decided not to answer that particular question. Anyway, it felt like one of those trick questions that teachers like to use. And so he pointed to the tray. "Your food is getting cold, Madam Mayor."

She gave him a penetrating look, then relented. "Think about my offer."

"I will," he said. "I'll discuss it with Jerry and let you know."

But as he walked out, he wondered if he should. Jerry wouldn't like it. Especially the part about the mayor knowing who they were, but also about the judge. For some reason,

Jerry was allergic to that judge and wouldn't enjoy the prospect of making the man's acquaintance again. Every time they did, they ended up in jail. Not that Johnny minded all that much. He actually enjoyed prison, but Jerry didn't. He fretted. And it's never a good idea to fret.

So he decided not to mention any of his conversation with their prisoner. What he would do was make sure she got a nice home-cooked meal next time. At least if he could convince Jerry to put in an effort. And if he couldn't, they could always order takeout. He knew just the place where they could get some great pasta.

CHAPTER 15

A meeting had been arranged and took place in Uncle Alec's office. For the occasion, his office had been transferred to what used to be the janitor's closet, since some construction was taking place in his own office. After a body had been discovered buried underneath that particular space, Alec had determined he didn't want to spend one more minute in there as long as that body hadn't been dug up and relegated to a proper graveyard. And so it was against the background noise of jackhammers that he tried to make his intention clear.

"I will not rest until we have found my wife and brought her abductors to justice!" he said, raising his voice to be heard over the noise. "If I have to bring in the National Guard, the Army, the State Police, the FBI: we will find her, and we will find her now!" And to show them that he meant it, he pounded his desk.

Odelia nodded. Her uncle was right. This was a crime of such brazenness that it couldn't be left unanswered. There had been kidnappers active in Hampton Cove before, but they had abducted their cats, not the mayor.

"What do you want us to do?" she asked now.

"I want you to talk to anyone who may have seen something," he said. "And start with all the stores located along Main Street, because I have it on good authority that Charlene's kidnappers used that as their escape route. At least seven bystanders who saw the whole thing say the van drove in that direction."

"I'll ask to see any CCTV from any of those stores," Chase suggested. "Get a license plate, maybe the identity of the driver if we're lucky."

Uncle Alec buried his face in his hands for a moment, and it was clear that the man was hurting. Which wasn't hard to understand. Odelia couldn't imagine how she would feel if her husband was abducted or, God forbid, her daughter.

"We'll get her back," she told her uncle. "I've told Gran to mobilize the cats, and they will mobilize every pet in town."

"Yeah, we'll get her back for you, Chief," said Chase.

He nodded morosely. "This is a nightmare," he announced.

The moment they left the office—or the janitor's closet—they headed straight for the main office so Chase could address the troops. All the officers were gathered there, and the gravity of the situation was mirrored in their expressions of utter focus and the utmost seriousness. And so Chase did what he did best: rally the troops and assign the various tasks to the officers present. Before long, the streets would be swarming with the boys and girls in blue, talking to every possible witness, confiscating every piece of CCTV footage, and digging through every last scrap of evidence that might point to Charlene's kidnappers.

The roads leading to and from Hampton Cove had all been barricaded, and every car passing through was being subjected to a thorough search. It was possible that the kidnappers had already left the area, of course, but if they hadn't, they wouldn't get far. A house-to-house search along Main Street was being organized, as well as an appeal in the paper and on social media for any witnesses to come forward. Hampton Cove was under siege, and no stone was being left unturned to find Charlene and bring her home safe.

She looked up as a helicopter circled overhead and hoped that when they did find Charlene, she would be all right. If not, her uncle would be devastated. And as she joined the rest of the team, talking to possible witnesses all along Main Street, she wondered how Max and the others were doing. He was her secret weapon, and frankly, she was relying on him and the others to bring this to an end.

We had arrived at the General Store, where we found Kingman looking perturbed.

"I was almost kidnapped," he announced. "Can you believe it? A guy actually tried to grab me."

"What a coincidence," I said. "Someone just went and kidnapped Charlene Butterwick."

"You don't say," said Kingman. It was rare for him not to be the first to know about a stunning event like that. "When did this happen?"

"About an hour ago. Gran told us. Apparently, they grabbed her when she walked out of Town Hall and shoved her into a van and then took off with her."

"Gee, I think I may have seen the kidnappers," said Kingman. "I saw a white van speeding down Main Street around that time. Johnny Carew was behind the wheel."

I shared a look of dismay with my friends. "You actually saw Carew behind the wheel of that van?" I asked.

"That's right. He seemed to be in a hurry, probably breaking the speed limit."

"Now why would Carew and Vale kidnap the mayor?" asked Brutus. "That makes no sense."

"Especially since they know her," I said. "And she will immediately recognize them."

"Not if they wear a mask," said Dooley. "Kidnappers always wear a mask to make sure their victims don't recognize them. Otherwise, they'll be in trouble when they release their victims."

"Look, there's something I wanted to talk to you guys about," said Kingman. "I've come to realize that I may need a bodyguard. I mean, I've been able to stop this guy from grabbing me, but what if he tries again? And this time maybe brings a friend? So I want to hire the four of you as my bodyguards. Make sure this doesn't happen again, you know."

"Did you recognize your attacker?" asked Brutus.

"I did, yeah. It was the same guy who was caught stealing. I caught him, and so now I think he's out for revenge. Which is why I'm not taking any chances. If he succeeds in grabbing me, it won't be for the ransom. He'll want to get rid of me!"

This was an extremely dangerous turn of events, and so we immediately agreed that we would act as his bodyguards. Now I don't really see myself as a bodyguard, per se, but there's strength in numbers, and this kidnapper would probably think twice when he was confronted not with one cat but five instead.

Just at that moment, Gran and Scarlett came walking into the General Store, looking very serious indeed. "Wilbur!" said Gran as she stepped into the store. "Wilbur, the watch needs you!"

Wilbur, who had been chatting up a female customer, who looked extremely relieved to be rid of him and now hurried out of the store as fast as her legs could carry her, gave Gran a look of annoyance. "What is it this time?"

"Charlene's been kidnapped," Scarlett pointed out. "And so it's our duty as the neighborhood watch to make sure she's found and brought home to her family."

This shut Wilbur up for a moment as he scratched his scalp. "I don't know what's happening today. First, Kingman almost got nabbed, and now Charlene?"

"Kingman almost got taken?" asked Gran.

"Yeah, by this guy I caught stealing this morning. Um, Sonny Hayworth, his name is. Always up to no good. So if I were you, I'd take a closer look at the guy. He probably took Charlene and can't wait to cash in on the ransom money."

"Duly noted," said Gran. "So you better close the store, and we'll get going."

"Close the store!" said Wilbur. "Are you nuts?"

"Didn't you hear me?" said Gran. "Charlene has been kidnapped!"

"So? People get kidnapped every day. Talk to the cops."

For a moment, Gran and Scarlett were too shocked to speak, then they both erupted into a long stream of words that are too saucy to print. The upshot was that Wilbur agreed to close early for the day and accompany his fellow watch members to go pay a visit to Mr. Hayworth and save Charlene from the man's grip.

"First, we need to pick up Francis," Gran said once the last customer had left the store.

"That's going to be hard," said Wilbur. "Francis is going to Rome."

"Rome can wait," said Gran. "Charlene can't. Now let's go!"

I wanted to tell her about Kingman witnessing Johnny Carew in his van speeding away, but didn't get the chance, as she and her fellow watch members suddenly made haste and were gone before I could stop them. And I couldn't even send her a message on her phone, since cats don't own smartphones. In that sense, we're like people from a bygone era: the smartphone-less era.

At least they'd go after Kingman's kidnapper, so that was something to be grateful for.

CHAPTER 16

Sonny had been watching from a small coffee shop across the street from the General Store, a cap pulled deeply over his eyes and sipping from a latte macchiato he couldn't really afford. Now that fat cat was joined by four more cats. A red one, a fluffy gray-beige one, a nice black specimen, and a perfectly gorgeous Persian. He wondered if customers of the General Store didn't find it annoying that a bunch of cats took up space in front of the store and meowed up a storm. It did add a wrinkle to his plans to grab that fatso and make a run for it.

Last time Kingman, as the creature was apparently called, had caught him by surprise. But that wasn't going to happen twice. As a professional, he had a reputation to uphold, and if his colleagues found out, or, God forbid, the people he worked for, that would put an end to his career.

His phone chimed and he quickly picked up.

"Sonny, your daughter wants to talk to you," said his ex-wife Valerie in the kind of cold and curt tones he'd become accustomed to from her.

"Hi, sweetie," he said when Kiki took over the phone from his mom.

"Daddy, I want to apologize that I didn't eat the spaghetti you made, especially after all the work you did. And I hope you didn't throw it away, because I would very much..." Here she paused for a moment, and he could hear furious whispering being carried on before she returned. "I would very much like to eat your spaghetti, since it's the very best in the whole wide world and it also happens to be my favorite dish."

Even though he knew that Valerie had put her up to this and had made her make the call, his heart still warmed. "Oh, that's so nice of you to say, sweetie," he said. "And as it happens, I do still have that spaghetti. I saved it in a Tupperware."

"Oh, yum," said Kiki without much conviction. "I'll drop by later, if that's all right. Then we can have dinner together and talk about how much I love you."

He smiled. Val had really done a number on her this time. "I love you, too, sweetheart. And I look forward to seeing you later tonight. Now can you put your mother on again?"

"Bye, Daddy."

"So she told you about the spaghetti, did she?" he asked his ex-wife.

"She did. And I think she even felt sorry. A little. Well, you know what she's been like lately. Turning into a real brat."

"She told me she's dating a sixteen-year-old kid who takes her on rides on his motorcycle."

"Oh, is that right?" said Valerie, and he could just imagine her giving their daughter a very critical look. "I'll have to talk to her about that, won't I? Thank you for letting me know." She lowered her voice. "What's the kid's name?"

"Um... Dean, I think."

"God, not that one. I told her to stay away from him." She

paused. "Maybe you can talk some sense into her? Or better yet, talk some sense into this Dean character. Put the fear of God into him. Make sure he never comes near Kiki again."

"I'll do just that little thing," he promised, the idea having briefly passed through his mind as well.

"Go do it now," she suggested. "I know where he lives."

The way she made it sound like a threat made him grin. "Is that a fact?"

"That is a fact. And if you go over there now, I might even invite you over for dinner next time I cook something really delicious. Though it won't be spaghetti, I can promise you that."

"Hey, don't knock my spaghetti. That happens to be my signature dish."

"So can you take care of the kid now?"

He hesitated.

"Don't tell me you're working again, Sonny."

"Of course I'm not working again. I told you I was going straight, didn't I?"

"It wouldn't be the first time you fed me a lot of nonsense."

"Okay, I'll go and talk to him now. But you gotta promise to invite me for dinner, all right?"

"I will," she said and sounded a lot less hostile already. It almost made him drop his plans to grab that fat cat belonging to Wilbur Vickery and wring his neck—the cat, not the guy. Though he wouldn't mind wringing Vickery's neck as well.

But since he'd made his ex-wife a promise, he dropped a couple of bills on the table, slipped down from his stool, and headed for the door. The things he did for his family.

* * *

"THAT'S HIM!" Kingman suddenly yelled, pointing to a man across the street. He had just walked out of that new coffee shop that had popped up there and had a cap drawn deeply over his eyes. "That's the man who tried to grab me!"

"Maybe we should follow him," Brutus suggested. "Make sure he doesn't try again."

"Or maybe you should stay very close to me," Kingman said. "And make sure he can't get at me!"

It certainly was a dilemma we were suddenly faced with. Furthermore, since we knew that Johnny Carew and Jerry Vale were merely guns for hire and had probably abducted Charlene at the instigation of a third party, maybe this man was that third party, and was eager to add Kingman to his list of victims.

"Let's follow him," I said therefore.

"Or I could stay here," said Harriet. "Protect Kingman? And then I could run some of my plans for cat choir by him. How does that sound?"

Kingman gave me a pleading look. 'Don't leave me here alone with her!' that look said. But since we had to move fast, I said, "Yeah, yeah, that's fine."

"I'll also stay here," said Brutus. "It's not safe for a girl alone," he added.

"Okay, all right," I said impatiently, and so when we finally moved out, it was just me and Dooley. By then, the guy who had tried to abduct our friend had a head start on us, so we hurried to catch up with him.

All along Main Street I saw cops talking to shopkeepers and the people that lived above the stores, looking for clues as to who might have kidnapped Charlene. I could have told them we were in pursuit of the likely kidnapper, but since humans rarely pay attention to what cats have to say, I knew it was no use trying to tell any of the officers we passed. And since I didn't see Odelia or Chase anywhere around, it looked as if it was up to us to catch this man and save Charlene.

CHAPTER 17

*V*esta, Scarlett, and a very reluctant Wilbur had arrived at St. John's Church to pick up the fourth member of their neighborhood watch so they could go full throttle in finding Sonny Hayworth and save the mayor's life. Vesta, never a patient person under the best circumstances, quickly lost her patience when, after ringing the bell at the rectory, no response came from inside. She decided to take a more proactive approach, as was her habit.

And so, first, she pounded on the unyielding door with her fist. It still wouldn't open. Then she resorted to repeating the same procedure on the windows, looking through them while shielding her eyes and peering inside. "I don't think he's home," she said finally.

"Of course he isn't home," said Wilbur. "I told you he was going to Rome. He probably left already."

"How can he do this to us!" Vesta cried in dismay. "Just when this town needs him the most, he's gone and taken a pleasure trip!"

"I doubt if going to Rome is a pleasure trip," said Scarlett. "Sounds to me like it's a business trip."

"Yeah, he probably was called there to meet the Pope or something," Wilbur opined. "Maybe get a promotion? You know what these big corporations are like. When the big boss summons you to headquarters for an urgent meeting, either it's because you're getting canned or you're moving up in the world."

"Francis did fool around with that girlfriend of his for a while," Vesta said thoughtfully. "So maybe he's getting reprimanded?"

"He already was reprimanded," Scarlett reminded her. "By the bishop."

"Well, upper management doesn't always know what lower management is up to, and vice versa," said Wilbur. "But anyway, are we gonna stand here twiddling our thumbs all day, or are we going to look for Sonny?"

"We'll look for Sonny," said Vesta resolutely. But then she thought she saw something inside the house that the parish had so graciously put at Francis Reilly's disposal. It looked like… "Hey, I think I saw someone moving around in there. Looks like…" It was hard to believe, but it looked like Shanille.

And since the last thing she could stomach was people deserting their beloved pets or subjecting them to any kind of torment, a righteous rage suddenly took possession of her. She picked up her phone and called Francis's number. She had already tried calling the man several times and had left several messages, but so far he had ignored them all—the calls and the messages. But now, as luck would have it, he picked up. He sounded a little out of breath, though, and nervous.

"What is it?" he said, and judging from the background noise, he was at the airport, just as Wilbur had suspected.

"We're standing in front of your place," she told him, "and

if my eyes aren't deceiving me, Shanille is inside, and you're not home. So what gives?"

"I'm at JFK," he said, confirming their suspicions. "I'm booked on a flight to Rome in half an hour. And I dropped Shanille off at the pet hotel, so it's impossible that she would be inside since I locked the place up before I left and told Mrs. Katerall not to come in for the next two weeks."

"You do realize that your town needs you, right? Mayor Butterwick has been abducted, and the neighborhood watch is on the case."

"I'm sorry, Vesta. I saw your messages, but I can't miss this flight. It's very important that I'm on it."

"So it's true, then, is it? The Pope has summoned you to come to Rome?"

"What? No, of course not. Father Luigi did. We met in the seminary and kept in touch. He's been inviting me to pay him a visit for years, and I finally decided to take him up on his offer. And I have to tell you, I'm really looking forward to it. He's going to show me the sights, and maybe we'll even get a glimpse of His Holiness. Look, I really gotta run, Vesta. They just called my flight."

"Wait—"

But he was gone. She gave her fellow watch members a funny look. "He's off to Rome."

"See? Told you," said Wilbur. "Off to see the big boss."

"It's nothing like that," she said and took another glance through the window. And this time she was sure of it: Shanille was in there, and she was trying to stay out of sight, ducking behind the table just as Vesta put her face against the glass. "That's it," she said determinedly. "I'm going in."

"What? But he just told you he's in Rome!" said Wilbur.

"Not yet, he's not," she murmured, only paying scant attention to Wilbur's protestations. The man should man up and get with the program. If the watch wanted to gain access to a place, it just went and did it. And so she hurried around the house, knowing the way since she'd been a guest at the rectory many times before. It didn't take her long to locate the spare key tucked away underneath a flower pot and use it to open the back door that led straight into the kitchen.

"Shanille!" she yelled. "I know you're in here, so there's no sense hiding from me, you hear! Ah, there you are," she said as the cat moved into view, looking distinctly nervous about this unexpected meeting. She crouched down with some effort and creaks of protest from her knees and gave the cat a stroke across the head. "Now what's going on here, huh? Francis just told me he dropped you off at the pet hotel. So did you escape or what?"

Shanille nodded, then suddenly burst into tears. "I was so sure he was going to take me to Rome with him. I was going to meet the Pope, and he was going to make me the next conductor of the Sistine Chapel Choir, and we were going to live there, and Francis was going to be the next Pope, and I was going to rule the roost and be a papal cat. And so when the cab arrived, I was sure it was going to take us to the airport, but instead it took us to this horrible place they call a pet hotel, and he just dumped me there! And then he left! I hate that man—I hate him, I hate him, I hate him!"

"Yeah, that wasn't a nice thing to do," Vesta agreed. "At the very least, he could have dropped you off at my place. I would have taken good care of you, honey."

"It's not just that. I told everyone I was leaving for Rome and I said goodbye, and now they'll know that I didn't leave, and it's going to be so humiliating!"

"Oh, I wouldn't worry too much about that if I were you," said Vesta. "I've humiliated myself so many times people have gotten used to it by now. And I'm sure your friends will be happy that you didn't leave. In fact, they'll be delighted."

"You really think so?"

"Of course! They are your friends, after all."

"Okay," said Shanille, wiping away her tears.

"So you escaped and came back here, huh? So what was the plan? That you were going to hide out here for the next two weeks until Francis returns from Rome?"

"Something like that. And I figured Matilda would find me, and make sure my bowls were filled and my litter box cleaned out. I don't like the pet hotel, Gran. It's a terrible place where they put us in cages, and we are only allowed to get out of them once a day to walk around before they lock us up again."

Vesta's expression hardened. "I'm sure Francis didn't know it was that bad, or he would never have put you there. But I'll make sure he knows. In fact, I'll make sure the whole world knows how they treat pets in that place. Anyway, you can't stay here all by yourself, hiding away like some leper. Why don't you go to my place? Your friends will be more than happy to share their home with you."

"I don't know about that," said Shanille. "Harriet won't be happy. And she'll gloat, I just know she will."

"If she does, she'll have me to deal with," said Vesta. "Okay, that's it. I will hear no more arguments from you, missy. You're coming with me right this instance."

Shanille gave her a grateful look. "Oh, Gran, you really are the best."

"And don't I know it!" said Vesta with a grin. "Just kidding. Let's get your litter box and your bowls and your favorite blanket and toys, and I'll drop you off at the house before I go look for the man who kidnapped Mayor Butterwick."

"Someone kidnapped Mayor Butterwick?"

"They did, and we know who did it."

"Of course you do," said Shanille.

Twenty minutes later, Shanille was set up at the house,

and the three remaining members of the neighborhood watch got back into the car to go look for Charlene. And as she stomped on the accelerator, the warm feeling spreading through her heart told Vesta that she'd gone and done a good thing today.

CHAPTER 18

It was with some trepidation that Johnny Carew returned to their prisoner, this time carrying another tray loaded with an actual home-cooked meal. Though truth be told, it hadn't exactly been cooked in their home but in the home of someone else entirely. Jerry's ex-wife, Marlene, had recently gone through a separation from her new husband, and in the process of that separation, she seemed to have had a remarkable change of heart about her first ex-husband, Jerry. Apparently, her new ex-husband had proven to be even worse than Jerry. And so now she and Jerry were on speaking terms again. So much so that she even cooked for them from time to time and made sure that Jerry, who she had called skin and bone, fattened up a little.

So when they asked Marlene if she could cook an extra meal for a guest of theirs, she had complied. From the smells emanating from said meal, Johnny actually hoped that Madam Mayor would refuse to eat it so he could do the honors himself.

He knocked on the door, then called out, "Are you decent, Madam Mayor?" When no answer came, he opened the door with the key and entered. The mayor was standing by the window looking out, and when he put this second tray on the table, replacing the first one, she gave him a frown. "I don't understand why you're doing this, Johnny. What have I ever done to you to deserve this, huh?"

He could have told her that her husband had put him behind bars several times in the recent and even the not-so-recent past, but he didn't want the atmosphere to turn acrimonious again, so he demurred from answering that particular question. "I think you will like this home-cooked meal, your honor."

She glanced at the meal but with a distinct lack of interest. "I mean, can't you let me go? I'll make sure it goes on your record that you treated me well."

"But it's for your own good, Madam Mayor!" he finally blurted out.

She gave him a look of surprise, then gestured to the bare walls and the ramshackle furniture. "This is for my own good? You'll have to explain that one to me, Johnny. Because from where I'm standing, this is all very puzzling."

Uneasy with himself that he had allowed himself this outburst, he decided to trudge ahead regardless. They always said that a happy prisoner is a good prisoner and gives their captors a lot less grief. So he figured that if he could make her see the reasoning behind this situation, she might relax and finally stop giving him such a hard time. And since Jerry had finally come clean and told him the whole story, he didn't see why he shouldn't share it with the mayor.

"It's like this, see," he said. "When a person loves another person, there are times when that second person thinks they've stopped loving the first person, even when the first person knows full well that isn't the case. And if only they can sit that second person down and talk to them, they'll finally see the light, see?"

Clearly, she didn't, for she just stared at him with that disconcertingly hard gaze she had, possibly earned through years of being in politics, a tough profession by all accounts, and one he personally didn't think he had the stomach for.

"Can you say that again, but in English this time?" she said.

"It's not me who should be saying all this. It's him." And feeling he'd already said too much, he gestured to the meal once more. "Don't let your food get cold."

"Johnny, wait!" she said, but he thought he'd heard Jerry coming down the corridor, and if the latter caught his partner chatting with the prisoner, he wouldn't be happy. And so he held up a hand and quickly left the room. She had food, she had water, and if she wanted to go to the bathroom, she only had to say so. There endeth his obligation toward this most annoying of prisoners.

Maybe that's why some kidnappers tied up their victims and used blindfolds and gags. At least they didn't get any lip from them!

He met Jerry in the corridor. "And? Any complaints?"

"No, she seemed to like the food," he lied.

"Good," Jerry grunted. "Marlene's food is the best. I've missed it, you know, while she was married to that no-good piece of work Billy Masterson."

"So when is this guy going to come and talk to the mayor?" he asked.

"Beats me. I guess he first wants to let her stew in her own juices for a while." He sincerely hoped this stewing in juices wouldn't go on for too long, but when he said as much to Jerry, he shrugged. "Who cares? The longer, the more money we're being paid, so it's all to the good. And now let's eat. I'm starving."

He stared at his friend. "Eat what? I gave everything to the mayor."

Jerry's jaw actually dropped. "You did what?!"

"Well, I thought—"

"How many times have I told you not to think, Johnny? I'll do the thinking. You just do as you're told. So now what are we supposed to eat, huh?"

"Maybe you can call Marlene and ask her to cook for us again?"

Jerry thought about that for a moment, then nodded. "I guess it is another opportunity for me to connect to the love of my life." And then an actual smile lit up his ferret-like features. They almost made his face look beautiful. Not really, though. The only way for Jerry to ever look palatable was if a plastic surgeon went to town on him, and even then he would have to be a very talented and courageous plastic surgeon—one who loved a challenge.

Jerry took out his phone and called Marlene. "Marlene, honey," he said in his most honeyed tones. "We loved the meal you cooked us so much we were wondering if by any chance you've got seconds?" He listened for a moment, then he said, "Spaghetti? Sure, I love spaghetti." He disconnected and gave his partner a smile. "It's in the bag."

CHAPTER 19

We had been following Sonny for a while now and had a hard time keeping up, as the guy seemed to be in something of a hurry. And since human legs are a lot longer than ours, we had to put in the occasional sprint to make sure we weren't left behind, which would have been a disaster.

"I hope," said Dooley between two pants from the exertion, "he will lead us straight to Charlene, Max."

"Yeah, I hope so too," I said.

"But when we get there, how are we going to save her? This guy probably has a gun."

"Not to mention accomplices," I said, if the Johnny and Jerry angle was for real. I had thought of this problem, and all I could say was, "We'll have to improvise."

"Okay, Max," said my friend, either showing how much faith he had in my capacity to improvise, or that he really was too out of breath to think of anything else to say.

We had arrived at what looked like a sort of playground for older kids, with basketball hoops where a couple of teenagers were playing a game of basketball. On the sidelines, more teenagers sat, looking either distinctly bored or smoking and looking at their smartphones. For some reason, they all seemed to suffer from an affliction also known as lacking a spine, in the sense that their bodies almost seemed draped on whatever surface they occupied. It was a physical phenomenon I had noticed before, especially with those of a young age. How people can survive without a spine, I don't know, but these kids seemed to be doing just fine.

Sonny now walked up to one of the kids hanging on the sidelines and suddenly, and quite out of nowhere, grabbed him by the collar, if a T-shirt has a collar—I could be thinking of a different garment—and started shouting something at him that didn't sound all that friendly.

"You're staying away from my daughter, is that understood!" he yelled at the kid, who looked sort of stunned to be attacked like this, quite out of the blue.

"What are you talking about, man?" the kid finally said.

"Kiki—I'm talking about Kiki!"

"But... I don't know any Kiki, bud."

"You are Dean, aren't you?"

"Nah. I'm Sean. That's Dean over there." He was pointing to a very tall and powerfully built kid who now stood with the basketball under his arm, darting a strange look at Sonny.

"You—you're Kiki's dad?" asked the kid as he approached.

Sonny blinked as he took in all of that muscularity. The kid was at least a head taller than he was and probably had at least fifty pounds on him.

"Y-yeah," he said, a lot less belligerent already.

"Bring it in!" said the kid suddenly, and wrapped Sonny in his arms and pressed him to his chest. "I've been dying to meet you. Kiki's dad, huh?" He actually lifted Sonny off the ground for a moment as he held him in a bone-crushing hug, then released him.

Sonny, hurt but not broken, wagged a tentative finger in

the kid's face. "You're to come nowhere near m-m-my daughter, is that understood?"

"Funny guy," said the kid affectionately. "I have the greatest respect for you, sir. I've been asking Kiki to introduce me to her mom and dad, so this is a nice surprise." He then held up the ball. "Hey, do you play?"

"I don't really… play," said Sonny, gulping a little as the rest of the kid's crew now all gathered around. And since they were all as tall and athletic as Dean, Kingman's would-be kidnapper blanched. "Maybe I'll take a rain check," he finally managed.

"Any time, sir," said Dean, that big goofy smile never leaving his lips. "Hey, I really love your daughter, you know. And I respect the hell out of her. Maybe you and Kiki's mom can meet my folks one of these days."

"Yeah, yeah," said Sonny, eager to get away. "Sure thing."

"I'll set it up," said Dean. He pointed to Sonny, who was now quickly walking away. "I love you, Kiki's dad. You're a real star!"

"You too," said Sonny as he hurried off.

"He's getting away, Max!" said Dooley, and so even though we had been able to take a short breather, the game was afoot once more, with us in pursuit and Sonny walking away as fast as his legs could carry him.

"I didn't see Charlene anywhere, Max," said Dooley.

"No, I didn't see her either," I said, wondering what was going on. Then again, even kidnappers have a personal life, and clearly Sonny was going through some issues with his daughter Kiki and the boyfriend he didn't approve of. And as we kept a close eye on the man, suddenly Sonny's phone belted out one of Taylor Swift's songs, and he picked up. "Yeah, what is it, Val?" he grunted into the device as he darted a quick look over his shoulders at Dean and his friends. "My spaghetti? You want me to give my spaghetti to your sister's ex-husband? Are you nuts?" But he quickly piped down. "Okay, all right, I'm sorry. Yeah, I shouldn't have said that. It's just that I talked to this Dean kid just now and things didn't exactly go as planned. No, he's actually not that bad. Very friendly kid. He even invited us to meet his folks." He held the phone away from his ear for a moment as he closed his eyes, and even we could hear the tirade bursting from the device.

"I don't think Val likes Dean," said Dooley.

"No, something tells me that she doesn't," I agreed.

The moment Sonny disconnected, he put in another burst of speed, and so it was all we could do to keep up with the guy.

"He's going to lead us straight to Charlene, Max," said Dooley. "I can feel it!"

CHAPTER 20

Kingman already felt a lot safer knowing that Brutus and Harriet were there to protect him in case Sonny returned. Wilbur had closed the store and hung up a sign indicating he'd be back soon, and so Kingman and his friends had retreated to the apartment upstairs, where they looked out of the front room window at the street below.

"It's a fascinating sight," Brutus said. "So many people."

"Yeah, you see the whole world go by," Kingman agreed.

He had positioned himself on the pillow that Wilbur had placed on the windowsill so he could look from his perch at the passersby on Main Street. It was one of his favorite pastimes the moment the store was closed, though of course he much preferred to be out there, where he could actually talk to cats. Then again, it was probably safer to be behind lock and key, where Sonny couldn't get to him.

"You know, I just saw the strangest thing," said Harriet. "I thought for a moment that I actually saw Shanille. Which is impossible, of course."

"You saw Shanille?" asked Brutus.

"Yeah, she was in Gran's car, and they were passing by here and going very fast, as if they were in a hurry. Gran and Scarlett were in the front, and Shanille was in the back with Wilbur. But that's impossible, since Shanille is supposed to fly to Rome today with Father Reilly."

"Maybe she missed her flight," said Kingman, who wasn't all that interested in Shanille and this whole cat choir business. He didn't care one bit who led the choir, as long as he got the chance to shoot the breeze with his fellow cats on a regular basis.

"Nice place you got here," said Brutus as he glanced around.

"It isn't much, but it's home," Kingman quipped. "You guys have never been up here?"

Brutus and Harriet shook their heads. "Only the store," said Harriet.

"Max and Dooley have," he said. "When we were being chased by a gang of kids. They followed us up here, and we had to jump out of the window to get away from them." He shook his head good-naturedly. "Crazy kids."

"I hope Max and Dooley will be all right," said Harriet with a touch of concern in her voice. It was the first time she'd decided to stray from her favorite topic of cat choir and give a moment's consideration to the fate of their friends, who were out there right now, putting their lives on the line for Charlene and Kingman both.

"They'll be fine," Brutus assured her. "Max is very clever, and Dooley… Well, Dooley is… I guess he is…" His face sagged. "Yeah, I really hope they're fine."

"You should have gone with them, tootsie roll," said Harriet. "We both know that Dooley is no match for that horrible man. And Max may be smart, but he's not really a fighter, is he? Not like you."

Brutus's chest swelled a little. "I guess you're right. Max and I make a formidable team. Unbeatable, I'd say."

Kingman listened to this conversation with a sense of amusement. "Look, if you really want to leave, just say so. I'm sure I'm fine by myself. It's not as if this guy can get at me now, since all the doors are locked."

Brutus and Harriet shared a look, then Brutus shook his head. "We're on bodyguard duty, Kingman, and I'd never leave my post."

"If this guy is as dangerous as you say he is," said Harriet, "breaking in here would be a cinch for him. So we better stay put and make sure you're safe."

"If you say so," he said, but in spite of his lighthearted response, he was secretly glad he wasn't alone. He might be the largest cat in Hampton Cove, but he was no hero and abhorred violence of any kind. Just then, there was a sort of rattle downstairs, and he immediately recognized the sound. It was his pet flap!

"There's someone in the house!" he told his friends.

"Stay behind me!" said Brutus. "And don't move!" He had assumed a pugilistic stance, fists up and ready to fight whoever this intruder could be.

For a moment, nothing stirred, then they thought they could hear silent steps on the stairs.

"He's coming!" said Harriet. "We should hide!"

"No, we are going to stand our ground!" said Brutus.

Kingman preferred Harriet's view on the matter, and his eyes were already darting around the room, thinking of a good hiding place. But then the intruder stuck his head in the door, and he recognized him as Buster, the cat belonging to Fido Siniawski from the corner hair salon.

"Oh, there you are," said Buster happily. "I thought I'd find you here."

"Buster!" said Kingman. "You almost gave us a heart attack!"

"Oh, I'm so sorry," said Buster, a little crestfallen. "It's just that when I saw the sign on the door, I figured I'd sneak around the back and see if you were home."

Behind Buster, more cats materialized. He recognized Tigger, Misty, Shadow, Missy and others. All of them had tiptoed up the stairs and now crowded into the living room.

"What are you guys doing here?" asked Brutus, relaxing his stance.

"It's cat choir, isn't it?" said Harriet with satisfaction. "You've all heard I'm taking over from Shanille, and you couldn't wait for your first rehearsal. Well, you'll be happy to know I'm ready to take my responsibility, and I'm still looking for a couple of assistants to do the actual work of leading the choir, and then we're all set. So be patient, dear ones, and you will be rewarded a thousandfold."

Buster gave her a strange look, then said, "We heard about Charlene Butterwick being kidnapped, so we figured we should probably do something to find her. So we wanted to resurrect Max's idea about the Baker Street Cats and were hoping you could lead the charge, Kingman."

"Me!" said Kingman, both greatly surprised but also honored to a degree.

"Well, you are Hampton Cove's feline mayor," said Buster. "So it only seems appropriate that you should lead the search for the human mayor."

Kingman smiled. "Oh, you guys. That's so kind of you to say. Of course I will lead the search effort."

Harriet's face had sagged, but she managed to hide her disappointment well. "Max and Dooley are in pursuit of Charlene's kidnapper as we speak," she announced, "but I'm sure they could use a helping paw."

"And if it's true that Johnny and Jerry were seen in the

area when Charlene was kidnapped," said Kingman, "they might be involved as well. So let's all spread out and find Charlene, shall we?"

"Oh, but not you, Kingman," said Brutus sternly. "Charlene's kidnapper wants to kidnap you, too, remember? It's much too risky for you to venture out there."

But he waved this reservation away with a gesture of his paw. "That's a risk I will have to take," he told his friend. "Charlene's life is in danger, so we should all be instrumental in securing her release. So are you all with me?"

A loud cheer rose up in the living room from the dozens of cats that had gathered there. And so he led the way out and down the stairs. Like a general leading his army, he actually felt pretty good about his new role.

Mayor Kingman. It did have a nice ring to it.

CHAPTER 21

I knew we were close when Mr. Hayworth entered an apartment building that looked as if it had seen better days, and for a moment, we were stumped.

"Now how are we going to save Charlene now?" asked Dooley.

"We have to get in there," I told him. "And find out where he is keeping her."

And as we thought of possible ways and means of entering this apartment building, which looked about as inviting to cats as the pound, a white van pulled up at the curb and Johnny Carew got out. When he caught sight of us, lurking across the street and keeping an eye on the building, he actually gave us a little wave and walked over for a chat.

"You're Odelia's cats, aren't you? Aren't you far from home right now? Did you get lost or something? If you want, I can give you a lift home in my van. But first, I have to pick something up. Just wait right there. I won't be long."

And as he crossed the street, Dooley and I looked at each other.

"No way am I going in a van with that man, Max!" he said.

"My sentiments exactly, Dooley," I confessed.

The last time we had seen Johnny Carew, he had been in the business of selling drugs to kids, and the time before that, he had actually kidnapped us and locked us up in cages in some old farmhouse. So we weren't exactly looking forward to making this man's acquaintance once again!

"We better get away before he catches us again," said Dooley, with a sad look at the apartment building. "At least now we know where they're holding Charlene."

Something told me that we shouldn't give up so easy, though. And as we were about to take our leave, I saw a familiar figure walking up to the apartment building and disappearing inside. It was none other than Muscles, the French bulldog who had been a guest at our house for a little while not so long ago.

"Muscles!" I called out, just before the door closed behind him.

He pushed it open again and looked out with a look of surprise on his wrinkly features. "Oh, Max!" he said. "And Dooley. What a pleasant surprise! Did you come to pay me a visit?"

We quickly crossed the street, after ascertaining that no cars were ready to turn us into cat fricassee, and joined him on the sidewalk. "We're actually here on official business," I told him. "Charlene Butterwick, the mayor of Hampton Cove, has been kidnapped. We followed her kidnapper all the way here, but we have no way of getting inside to find Charlene."

"Do you live here now?" asked Dooley, happy to see our good canine friend.

"Yeah, the Schoenburgs had to sell the house to pay for all their legal bills and to pay back Otto's victims, so Otto's son relocated here with his family. It's not too bad, you know.

Not like the old place, of course, but at least those dreadful Dobermans are nowhere to be found."

"What happened to them?" I asked.

"Oh, they were adopted and shipped off to Alaska with their new owners. And good riddance, I say."

Muscles's human, Otto Schoenburg, was serving a long stretch in prison, and so his son, Jake, had adopted his dad's beloved canine. Muscles seemed to enjoy life with his new adoptive family, for he looked happy and healthy.

"You know, if you tell me this guy's name, I'll tell you what floor he's on and show you how to get up there," said Muscles now. "We developed this code, you see. Jake will let me out of the apartment, and since we live on the ground floor, I don't even need to take the stairs—which I hate, by the way—bad for the hips—and then when I've done my business, I walk back in and give the buzzer a nudge. Easy peasy."

And to demonstrate how it was done, he pushed open the door with his head, then showed us where Jake had installed a bell that he could reach. He nuzzled it, and immediately the door made a buzzing sound, and he pushed his way right in.

"The stairs are that way," he said. "And the elevator is that way. But I wouldn't recommend the elevator as it keeps breaking down." He shrugged. "The building is a little dilapidated, but Jake has promised us that he's working his fingers to the bone to get us all out of here soon and back to something a little more suitable for a family. And I believe him, you know."

The trial had shown that Otto's son was never involved in his dad's criminal empire and that, instead, he made a living in an honest way as an actuary. But since he had been implicated in his father's crimes, obviously money was tight right now. But that didn't seem to bother Muscles.

"To go out, you simply press that button," he said, indicating another button at his level that we could easily push. "Paul made the building canine proof," he said with a wink. "He's very creative like that."

"And very considerate," I said. "Not all dog owners would go to these lengths."

"What can I say? The guy loves me," he said with a grin. "And I guess I'm starting to warm to him as well," he added. "Just kidding. I'm crazy about these people. The salt of the earth—in spite of what others might think."

And since he figured we might not find where we needed to be, he decided to brave that staircase and show us the way. Before long we had started our long trek up the stairs, in search of Charlene's kidnapper and hopefully the place where he was holding her as a prisoner.

CHAPTER 22

*V*esta, Scarlett and Wilbur had dropped off Shanille at the house and were finally ready to go in search of Charlene when Vesta caught sight of Fifi, who sat on the sidewalk looking entirely forlorn.

"Hey, what's the matter with you?" asked Vesta as she bent over to give the Yorkshire terrier a pat on the head. She wasn't a dog person, per se, but that didn't mean she was against dogs, especially little sweethearts like Fifi.

The dog barked a sad sort of bark, but since Vesta didn't speak her language, she couldn't understand what she was saying.

"She's traumatized," said Shanille, who had popped out from behind the house and had listened in on their conversation. "Isn't that right, Fifi?"

Fifi seemed to nod in confirmation and gave a few more barks.

"Yeah, she says she saw a dead body this morning, and she's feeling very strange. Like weak and kinda sad. She doesn't know what's wrong with her, but she can't stop thinking about what she saw."

"Oh, the poor thing," said Vesta. "Maybe she should see a pet shrink?"

Shanille gave her a strange look. "Does that even exist?"

"Of course, it does. They've got regular shrinks for humans who've suffered a traumatic event, and pet shrinks for pets."

Shanille listened as Fifi became more talkative. "She says that Kurt made an appointment with a shrink," she said. "But obviously she can't go herself."

"We'll see about that," said Vesta as she picked up the little doggie. She turned to her fellow watch members. "I'm taking this dog to the vet. It's an emergency."

"I thought we were going to look for Charlene," said Wilbur, who looked bored.

"First things first. This poor doggie witnessed a violent crime this morning, and she's feeling all discombobulated. So it's urgent that we take her to see a pet shrink."

And since the only one in town who approximated this job description was Vena, she was taking her to see her. She knew that she probably should let Kurt decide, but then the poor guy was probably so traumatized himself he wasn't thinking straight.

And so they all hopped back in the car and she took off, yelling through the window to Shanille, "If anybody asks, we're at Vena's, all right?"

"All right, Gran," said Shanille with a surprised flick of her tail.

Before long they had reached the vet's offices on Grant Street and she got out. Since Scarlett and Wilbur refused to sit around while she paid a visit to the vet, they accompanied her in. As luck would have it, they were the only ones there, so Vena could see them immediately.

"Fifi witnessed a violent crime this morning," she

explained. "And a man who died as a consequence. And I think she's feeling traumatized."

Vena didn't ask how she knew this, nor did she have to, since at this point more or less everyone in town knew that Vesta, her daughter, and granddaughter had a 'thing' with cats, in the sense that they seemed to be able to understand what they said. They called them cat whisperers, and even though Fifi wasn't a cat, it went without saying that their gift might extend to other species of pets as well.

"Let me see what we've got here," said Vena as she lifted the doggie onto her table. She did a quick examination to establish whether physically she was in good health, and then said, "I can recommend you a pet shrink if you like. I've heard that she works wonders with pets, so you could always give it a try."

"Do it," said Vesta. "This dog needs to receive specialist care."

And so Vena wrote down the name, address, and telephone number of the shrink in question, whose name was Doris Twist, and Vesta took the note and thanked the vet.

Moments later, they were back in the car and she was driving to the address indicated, with Scarlett giving directions as read from the GPS app she liked to use.

"I hate to sound like a broken record," said Wilbur from his position in the backseat, "but when are we going to start looking for Charlene? I'm losing business here, you know."

"Later," she said. "First things first. And this dog is hurting, can't you tell?"

Wilbur stared at the mutt and shook his head. "Pet shrinks. What are they gonna come up with next? Pet massage parlors? Pet restaurants? Pet bars?"

"Hey, that's not such a bad idea," said Scarlett. "I bet that there are plenty of folks out there who would love to visit a pet restaurant or a pet bar."

"Oh, for crying out loud," Wilbur grumbled.

It didn't take them long to arrive at their destination, which was a nice villa in a peaceful neighborhood with plenty of similar dwellings. They got out, and Vesta rang the doorbell, holding Fifi in her arms. The door opened, and a wizened old lady appeared, who glanced from Vesta to Scarlett to Wilbur and then to Fifi. The moment her eyes, which were a little rheumy, landed on the fluffy little Yorkie, they lit up with delight.

"Oh, isn't she the cutest?" Fifi barked once, and the old lady clasped her hands together with perfect glee. "And polite, too!"

Vesta shared a look with her friend. Looked like this woman could actually talk to dogs! How about that?

They explained the situation, and Mrs. Twist said she charged sixty bucks for a session, but the first session was free, just to see if things gelled between herself and the patient. They took a seat in the waiting area while Doris took Fifi with her to the consultation room. Vesta caught a glimpse of a couch where the pet could lie, and a chair where the shrink could sit, and figured Fifi was in good hands.

"This is just a complete waste of time," Wilbur grumbled.

"Oh, will you shut up," said Vesta, "Fifi's well-being is very important to me, and if she doesn't get over this trauma she suffered, I wouldn't forgive myself if I hadn't done everything I could to make sure she was taken care of."

"But what about Charlene!" he said, waving his arms.

"Charlene can wait," she determined. "And besides, this guy Sonny Hayworth won't harm a hair on her head if he knows what's good for him."

"It stands to reason," Scarlett argued, "that kidnappers have to take good care of their kidnappees, or else they won't get any money for them."

"But what if he cuts off one of her fingers? Or her ear or

something!" Wilbur cried. "Trust me when I tell you this guy Sonny is no sweetheart. He's bad news. Just ask your son."

But Vesta pressed her lips together. "First things first. Once Fifi has had her session and she's feeling better, then we'll think of Charlene and her fingers."

"Or her nose," Scarlett added as she touched her own appendage.

Wilbur was right, of course. They had to get cracking on this abduction business. But she couldn't just let Fifi suffer, could she? In her heart of hearts, it might even be said that she almost cared more about Shanille and Fifi's well-being than her daughter-in-law's, but then Charlene could take care of herself and Fifi and Shanille could not. Therein lay the difference.

"It's just that..." Wilbur suddenly looked nervous. "As long as we don't catch this guy, he might come after my Kingman, you know."

Vesta smiled and patted the man's knee. "Don't you worry about Kingman. He's got dozens of friends who will protect him. In fact, Kingman probably has more friends than you do, Wilbur."

Wilbur only looked slightly relieved by this statement. "If you say so."

He might be a grouch and a grump, but clearly the man had his heart in the right place if the well-being of his precious feline was so important to him.

The hour passed quickly, and when the door opened and Fifi came out with the shrink, she already looked a lot happier than when they had arrived.

"She'll be all right," said Doris. "This was her first dead body, you know, so it came as a great shock to her. A few more sessions and she'll be right as rain." Fifi barked once, and the old lady laughed. "No, thank you!" she said and let them out.

"Do you offer the same service to cats?" she asked.

"I do," said Doris. "So please drop by any time."

Something told her that Max, Dooley, Harriet and Brutus wouldn't be all that keen on this lady's particular services, but then you never know.

So they thanked Mrs. Twist and hurried back to the car so they could drive Fifi home again. It was time to start looking for Charlene Butterwick!

CHAPTER 23

With the assistance of Muscles, it didn't take us long to arrive on the designated floor. "You could have stayed with us, you know, Muscles," said Dooley as we made our way upstairs. "We all loved having you around."

"I know, Dooley," said the bulldog. "I loved staying with you, but at the end of the day, and for better or worse, the Schoenburgs are my family. Okay, so we don't always see eye to eye, but that's what families are like, isn't it? Sometimes you get along, sometimes you don't, but overall, you love each other, right?"

Dooley thought about this for a moment. "But... I always get along with my family, Muscles. And I always love them."

Muscles grinned. "That probably makes you the exception that proves the rule, buddy."

We had arrived on the third floor, where according to Muscles, Sonny lived. And since most homeowners don't respond to cats when they come calling—and besides, we're not tall enough to reach the doorbell—he showed us a neat trick. Along the outside of the building, a balcony ran, and since all of the apartments had the same balconies, you could easily jump from one to the next.

"Here, I'll show you how it works," he said, and pushed open the door that led outside. He was right: there was indeed a balcony, which, like the rest of the building, had seen better days, with paint chipped off and even parts of the concrete having crumbled to reveal the steel rods underneath. I gulped a little as I questioned whether the balcony wouldn't suddenly collapse and crash down to the sidewalk below, crushing some unfortunate passerby and us in the process.

"Is it safe, you think?" I asked.

"Oh, perfectly safe. It may look as if it's falling apart, and maybe it is, but it won't collapse just yet. At least if you don't go crazy and start jumping up and down."

And so when we set paw on the thing, we did so very, very carefully.

"Think light thoughts, Max," Dooley advised. "When you think light thoughts, it will make us very light and then the balcony won't even know we're here."

"Light as a bird," I murmured, therefore taking his advice to heart.

"Light as a feather," Dooley said, as a variation on the same theme.

"Light as a..." Muscles frowned. "Help me out here, you guys. What else is light?"

"Um... an airplane?" Dooley suggested.

"Airplanes are pretty heavy," I told him.

"Okay. So maybe... light as a light bulb?"

"Let's just do this," Muscles suggested, and trudged out ahead of us, used a chair to climb up, and then disappeared on the other side. Moments later, his head reappeared. "It's doable," he announced. "Just make sure you don't step on the bag."

I wondered what he meant with these mysterious words, but still did as he said. And so we both hopped up onto the chair that a kind soul—or possibly a cigarette smoker—had placed there for our convenience, then up onto the dividing wall and down... on top of a garbage bag filled with leftovers.

"Yikes!" said Dooley, much dismayed. "Now who puts a bag here?"

"They probably weren't expecting visitors," I told him.

We shook off the pizza boxes and empty hamburger wrappers and joined Muscles near the door, which offered a great view of the kitchen. "And there you go," he said, with the air of a tour guide who's finally reached the summit of the Eiffel Tower. "Sonny Hayworth, as I live and breathe."

"And Johnny Carew," said Dooley as we watched the scene with a sense of astonishment.

"Who's the girl?" I asked.

"Sonny's daughter," said Muscles. "She lives with her mom but visits her pop from time to time. There's usually a lot of shouting when she pays him a visit."

There was a lot of shouting now, as the girl sat eating what looked like spaghetti while Sonny wrapped up the same dish into a plastic tub, possibly for Johnny to take along.

"I didn't know he was into takeaway these days, though," said Muscles as we studied the scene from our vantage point. "But then he's always strapped for cash. Rumor has it that he's some kind of ex-con and that he's into all kinds of illegal schemes. At one time, he even used to work for Otto," he said, referring to his mobster human who was now serving a long stretch in prison.

"Thanks so much for this, Sonny," said Johnny jovially as he held up the plastic tub. "I won't forget this."

"Tell Jerry that he owes me," Sonny growled. "And that if I hadn't turned down that job, he wouldn't have landed it in the first place." He darted an eye at his daughter, then lowered his voice. "How is your guest, by the way? She behaving?"

Johnny's face sagged. "She's not happy. And her list of demands seems to be growing by the minute. A very difficult guest, this one. She doesn't like takeout, she doesn't like the stuff Marlene cooked up, even though it smelled delicious. So let's hope your spaghetti hits the spot, or else I don't know what to give her."

"You're much too easy, Johnny," said Sonny. "You should have put your foot down from the beginning. Make it clear that you're not running a five-star hotel. She'll pipe down soon enough."

"I know, but the whole setup appeals to my romantic nature," said Johnny. "I know Jerry will say I'm a hopeless romantic, but for two sundered hearts to come together again like this..." He smiled. "It's just so beautiful, you know. I can't wait for the big reunion to finally take place."

Sonny gave him an odd look. "It's just a job, Johnny. Get emotionally involved like this and you're doomed. So my advice? Just treat it like another job."

"That's what Jerry keeps telling me," said Johnny ruefully. "How is Valerie, by the way?"

"Valerie is fine," said Sonny, with another quick glance at his daughter, who clearly was not a big fan of her dad's spaghetti. "So Jer and Marlene are on speaking terms again, huh? Is he still so hung up on his ex-wife?"

"Oh, yes, he is. He's still hoping she will change her mind and they'll get back together one of these days."

"I know the feeling," said Sonny. " But those Markell sisters are tough. Once they're done with you, that's it. No second chances. You're out on your ear and they won't change their minds. And besides, Marlene has moved on."

"She has? I didn't know about that."

"Sure. She met this museum director or something. Runs

our local natural history museum. Real bookish type. Val keeps telling her he's not her type, but Marlene insists that after all the losers she's dated, she wants to try something new."

"That *is* a big change," said Johnny, scratching his scalp.

"Better don't tell Jerry. He'll go berserk."

Johnny nodded. "He still loves her, you know."

"I know," said Sonny, and it was clear that he sympathized. I got the impression that he still loved his wife, too. "But at some point, you gotta accept that it's over and move on, you know." He clapped the big guy on the back. "Tell Jerry I said hi."

"I will," said Johnny, a happy smile now creasing up his lips. The big lug never could stay down long. He might be a crook, but of all the crooks we had ever met, and we had met our fair share of them, he was by far the most congenial one.

And so he took his container with spaghetti and turned to leave. But just then, he caught a glimpse of the three of us staring intently through the window.

"Now will you look at that!" he said, a goofy expression sliding up his face. "It's those cats again—Max and Dooley. And they've found a funny little friend!"

Sonny now jerked his head around to take us in, and his eyes narrowed when he spotted us. Contrary to his colleague, he did not look happy to see us!

"Uh-oh," said Muscles. "I think we better skedaddle, lickety-split!"

And as Sonny set foot for the door that led to his balcony, the three of us hurried back to where we came from. It wouldn't do to be caught, especially considering the way he had treated Kingman.

"Come back here!" Sonny shouted as he tried to make a grab for us. But fortunately for us, we were quick off the mark, and had already scaled that wall before he got a hold of us. "Filthy vermin!" he shouted, which wasn't very nice, I thought. "Stay away from me, you hear!"

"You shouldn't keep food on your balcony, Sonny," we heard Johnny berate the man. "Everyone knows it will attract cats. They love that kind of thing."

We hurried back inside, and then down the stairs, hoping to arrive downstairs before Johnny got there. We thanked Muscles profusely, and the large bulldog took it in stride. "Glad to be of service, fellas," he said happily. "And whenever you're in the neighborhood, feel free to drop by, all right?"

"Of course, Muscles," said Dooley, and gave the bulldog a cuddle.

A couple of old ladies did a double-take when they witnessed the scene, then quickly took out their smartphones to take a picture.

I guess that rumored enmity between cats and dogs is highly overrated.

CHAPTER 24

Arriving outside, we found ourselves faced with two different white vans. I hadn't noticed before that Johnny's van was so nondescript that it closely resembled every other white van out there in the world, which probably was the whole idea of employing an 'unmarked white van' for nefarious purposes.

"Which one is Johnny's, Max?" asked Dooley.

"I have no idea," I confessed as we studied both vehicles closely.

Our general, and quite frankly sort of nebulous, idea had been that once Johnny crawled back into his van, unbeknownst to him, two illegal passengers would be located in the back of that van, hitching a ride and secretly discovering the place where he had hidden Charlene.

For it had now become quite clear to us that it wasn't Sonny who had abducted Uncle Alec's wife but Johnny and Jerry, even though Sonny was clearly involved somehow.

"Okay, so I think we'll have to go with our gut instinct here, Max," said Dooley. "So I'm picking..." He closed his eyes for a moment as his right front paw hovered in the air.

"I'm picking that one," he finally said, pointing to the left van. "What do you think?" he said, giving me an expectant look, like a show horse looking at its master after it has performed an exceptionally complicated trick.

"I think you called it, buddy," I said. Since I had absolutely no idea which one of these vans could possibly belong to Johnny, I figured we might as well allow chance and fate to guide us, or in this case, Dooley's gut instinct. And also, the van on the left was the only one of the two with a back door that wasn't fully closed, so it stood to reason it was also the only one we'd be able to hitch a ride in.

It wasn't long before we had secured a nice place underneath a convenient tarp in that van, and waited patiently—or not-so-patiently—for the next developments.

"Who would have thought that Johnny and Jerry were capable of kidnapping Charlene, Max?" said Dooley. "I thought they would have learned their lesson by now."

Over the course of our acquaintance with the two crooks, they had pulled a lot of stunts, but kidnapping the mayor of their town was definitely a first.

"Maybe they're expecting an exceptionally big payday," I suggested. "And the lure of all that money made them temporarily blind to the consequences of their rash act."

"Johnny said something about romance, though, didn't he? What was that all about, Max?"

"I have no idea, buddy. Maybe Jerry has fallen in love with Charlene and wants to make her love him by holding her prisoner?"

"Does that work, Max?" asked Dooley.

"Only in bad romance novels," I said.

There had been a movie on TV the other day where a man kidnapped a woman and held her prisoner, saying he'd only release her once she had grown to love him. Chase thought it was a load of nonsense, while Odelia said there might be something in that. Frankly, I very much doubted even she would enjoy being kidnapped by some random fellow and then forced to love him. Then again, as I think we've ascertained by now, humans as a species are a little weird.

"It's taking him an awfully long time, Max," said Dooley.

"He's probably tasting that spaghetti to make sure it's safe for human consumption."

But then finally something did stir. The door to the driver's cabin was opened, and the van moved as Johnny's bulk hoisted itself into the driver's seat, and he slammed the door shut. Moments later, the van's engine rumbled to life with a few coughs and roars, and before long, the van lurched into motion and we were off.

"It's happening, Max!" said Dooley. "We're going to find Charlene and save her life!"

It wasn't long before the van pulled to a stop again, and the engine was turned off. It amazed me that Charlene would be held so close to town, which told me that these two kidnappers were taking an enormous risk in doing so.

We waited another minute or so to make sure this was it, and then carefully pushed open the door again, which I now saw was held together with a piece of electric wiring to keep it from opening up all the way. As we poked our heads out, much to our surprise, we found ourselves back where we had been that morning.

"But... it's Sherlock Holmes's house!" said Dooley.

"It is," I said, astonished by the coincidence.

Was it possible that Johnny and Jerry were behind this tragic incident as well? But surely they wouldn't have brought Charlene here, would they? After all, the place had been crawling with cops all morning, and even now, yellow crime scene tape cordoned off the front door.

But since there was no trace of Johnny, it stood to reason

he must have entered the house to finish whatever job he had come there to do. And so we hurried across the front lawn, then around the back of the house and saw that Johnny had gained access to the house from the back door, which had been forced open.

"Did he use a key, you think, Max?" asked Dooley.

I studied the demolished lock and shook my head. "More like a crowbar."

"That's one way of getting in," Dooley agreed as he eyed the destruction.

For a moment, we paused on the doorstep, but since we were on a mission to save Uncle Alec's wife, we decided that fear and trepidation had no place in our plans. So, we ventured inside, hoping to find our beloved mayor and save her life from these two wretches.

It didn't take us long to determine where Johnny was, since we heard a lot of stomping around upstairs, with dust motes fluttering down from the ceiling as Johnny made no attempt to conceal his presence.

And so we moved ever so stealthily up those stairs to take a peek at what he was up to. As we raised our heads above the landing floor, we suddenly became aware of a singular fact: Dooley's gut had deceived us. The man going from room to room and making such an enormous racket wasn't Johnny. It was Sonny!

CHAPTER 25

"Looks like we were wrong all this time, Max," Dooley whispered.

"Yeah, looks like," I agreed.

What were the chances, though, for both Johnny and Sonny to own the same type of van? Then again, possibly this was the model all criminals used. Just like rich people all like to own the latest Tesla, and all royals want to own the latest Range Rover, in the criminal underworld they all wanted to possess the latest unmarked white van. It's all about fashion, after all, and showing off to one's peers that your pockets are so deep you don't have to stint for anything.

Sonny was certainly meticulous about his work, as he turned one room inside out before moving to the next one, where he repeated the procedure.

"He's making a big mess, Max," said Dooley quietly.

"He certainly is," I agreed. "The police won't be happy." Or Alan Gerard's relatives.

"Shouldn't there be a police officer guarding the scene?"

"They're probably too busy looking for Charlene right now to bother with guarding a crime scene," I said. Though they should have posted at least one officer to make sure that whoever had attacked Mr. Gerard looking for loot didn't come back to finish the job, as Sonny was now clearly in the process of doing.

"What is he looking for?" asked Dooley. But then he got it. "Oh, I know! He's looking for the same thing I was looking for before! Sherlock's pipes!"

"I very much doubt that, Dooley," I said. "Mr. Gerard's pipes probably aren't worth a great deal, if he ever owned a pipe in his life, that is." After all, pipes are not as popular as they used to be. Though they could always make a comeback, of course. Just like beards and mustaches seem to move in and out of style, maybe pipes would suddenly find a new audience among cool young hipsters.

Clearly, Sonny's search wasn't going well, for he kept grumbling to himself and his efforts to search for whatever it was that he was looking for became more and more erratic and frantic, associated with more and more violence and things being thrown around. At a certain point, he even roared like a lion, startling us both, and something came whizzing over our heads and crashed against the wall behind us.

We looked back and saw that it was a chair.

"He's not happy, Max," said Dooley, which was quite the understatement.

"If he targeted Mr. Gerard this morning," I said, "trying to make him tell him the hiding place of whatever he was looking for, and he's not finding it now, he must be desperate," I said. Which made Sonny a very dangerous man indeed.

"At least he makes good spaghetti," said Dooley, who looked quite scared now.

The man now came stomping out of the room he'd demolished, and judging from his red face, quick breathing, and sweat running down the side of his face in rivulets, things weren't going well for him. Then he suddenly directed a look at the ceiling and frowned. Moments later, he had pulled down the extendable ladder and was stomping up before disappearing into the gaping black hole.

"An attic, Max!" said Dooley. "Why didn't I think of that!"

For a few moments, we heard plenty of stumbling and mumbling and groans of frustration, but then suddenly, all of that stopped, and for a long moment, there was nothing. Not a single sound. Then: "Yahoo!"

"I think he found the pipes!" said Dooley.

"Whatever he found, it must be good," I said.

"You've got to hand it to Sherlock, Max. He hides his treasure well. Probably in some secret compartment hidden in a secret space hidden in his secret attic."

Whatever it was, the man now returned, looking much happier than before, even smiling to himself, which was the first time we saw that he actually possessed teeth. And as he clutched some object in his hand, we did our utmost to see what it was. It looked like a small package wrapped in brown paper.

"Those must be Sherlock's pipes," said Dooley reverently.

"And I think we better get out of here," I said in return.

And so we hurried back down those stairs before we were caught and turned into spaghetti sauce. And as our quarry followed our lead and descended the stairs, we watched him from behind a door leading to one of the rooms. It took me a little while to realize that this was the exact room where poor Mr. Gerard had breathed his final breath. Dooley must have come to the same conclusion, for he suddenly emitted an audible intake of breath. And then, of course, the worst happened: Sonny must have heard, and he looked up as if stung.

For a moment, he simply stood looking around, but then finally, he fixated a pair of beady eyes on us. Even though I could have sworn we were well concealed in the darkness of that room, the man must have sharp eyes, for he still saw us!

"And if it ain't those filthy rats again!" he growled and suddenly took a step in our direction. So Dooley and I immediately fled, hiding deeper in that room and scooting underneath a conveniently nearby couch. "Where are you!" he bellowed. "Always causing trouble for me! Come out from wherever you're hiding!"

But we had no intention whatsoever to comply with his urgent request. Instead, we simply remained perfectly still, not moving and not making a sound.

"I know you're in here," he said, malice creeping into his voice. "And I'll get you! Just like I'll get that nasty fat friend of yours, if it's the last thing I do! I'll get him, and then I'll wring his neck and turn him into cat stew! Or maybe I'll turn him into meatballs and serve them to my daughter or that boyfriend of hers."

As he searched everywhere for us, suddenly I caught sight of the package he had placed on the floor. And since curiosity is my middle name, I couldn't help but stick my head from underneath that couch to take a look.

"Max, no!" Dooley hissed.

I glanced up and saw that Sonny was checking behind the curtains now. So I sneaked up to that package and lifted a flap of that brown paper to look inside. For a moment, I didn't understand quite what I was seeing. But then I got it. It was a sunflower. Or in fact, several sunflowers. It was a painting.

But then suddenly, Sonny whirled around, and for a moment, our eyes met, and the world came to a full stop. "Dooley, run!" I yelled.

And as Sonny lunged for me, we both scooted from that room and ran as fast as we could—which I can tell you is considerably faster than any hundred-yard-dash athlete! And before Sonny could catch us, we were out of the house and racing through the backyard to hide in the bushes lining that strip of lawn.

And as we watched, Sonny came storming out, grabbing his precious package under his arm and shaking his fist.

"I'll get you!" he yelled at no one in particular. "You can run, but you can't hide from me! Sooner or later, I will find you, and I will turn you into meatballs!"

CHAPTER 26

The dinner rush had come, and along with it, the business that was part and parcel of running a successful restaurant. Roger, who had been on his feet almost since dawn, was starting to feel the fatigue taking hold of him but was determined not to allow it to diminish his focus. Attention to detail as well as an excellent product were the hallmarks of the Hungry Pipe, and he wasn't going to drop the ball. So far, there had been no more complaints or strange mishaps, and as he stirred his trademark fish sauce until it had the perfect texture and taste, he checked the clock and wondered if they'd make it till closing time without any major disaster.

He'd been keeping a close eye on Marco, who occupied his own section of the kitchen and ruled it as if it were his personal domain, which in a sense it probably was. Ever since the sous-chef had joined them, he'd been chipping away at Roger's throne bit by bit, undermining him in front of the other kitchen staff and even going so far as to openly criticize some of his decisions. Every other chef would have terminated his contract, but in this case, that was not an option he had. Marco was good. In fact, he was so good some people were starting to wonder if he was the future and Roger the past. But before that happened, Roger was ready to put up a fight.

He glanced at the serving table where the dishes were being placed before the servers went out and took them out to the diners. And that's when he saw it: someone had spilled a substance on one of the plates. It was a dark substance that had no business being there. And as his heart sank like a stone, he was at the table in two steps and closely studying the plate. He picked it up and dug his finger into the substance, then, after a moment's hesitation, took a taste.

It tasted like nothing he'd ever tasted before. Bitter and with a distinct aftertaste. It certainly wasn't part of the menu. When Ludo came bursting in through the swing doors, in great haste as usual, he immediately asked, "How many of these have you taken out here?"

Ludo gave him a puzzled look.

"How many!"

The young server snapped out of it. "Um... about half a dozen? It's our most popular dish, chef."

He closed his eyes in dismay then opened them again to give his server a furious look. "And you didn't notice this?" he said, pointing to the yucky substance spilled all across the rim of the plate.

"I... I just figured it was a new secret sauce?" he ventured, looking terrified now.

"And you didn't think to ask?!" he thundered, and actually grabbed the guy by the lapels and shoved him up against the wall. "You did this, didn't you?!"

"No, chef!" the kid cried.

Kirsten now came running in from the restaurant. "What's going on here?" she demanded. When she saw the scene, she immediately put her hand on her husband's arm. "Let go of him, Roger. Let go of him now!"

Reluctantly, he let go of the server, who practically dropped to the floor before he recovered. He looked at Roger as if he'd lost his mind, which maybe he had.

"Someone put this on my plates!" he said, pointing to the strange substance. "And what I would like to know—what I DEMAND to know is what it is, and who put it here. Cause it sure as heck wasn't me!"

All of the kitchen staff now stood around them, except Shonna, who was busy cooking up something that needed her constant eye lest it was ruined. But she did dart anxious glances in their direction.

Marco now dug his little finger into the substance and had a taste. He made a face. "But, chef," he said. "This is bird poop!"

He stared at the man. "Bird poop? Are you sure?"

"Absolutely." He gave them an embarrassed smile. "And if you ask me how I know what bird poop tastes like, as a kid, I once ate some of it as an experiment. As a, what do you Americans call it? A dare, yes, that's what it was. My best friend dared me to taste the poop of a pigeon and I did. And it tasted exactly like this."

Inadvertently, all of their eyes now rose to the ceiling, to make sure there wasn't a bird sitting on one of the light fixtures and defecating on their precious dishes. But as far as Roger could tell, there wasn't a single pigeon in evidence. Which meant…

"Someone put this on my dishes!" he roared. "So whoever it was, better confess right now, or I will have you filleted and shoved into the oven and served up with watercress. Is that understood?"

Kirsten, who had a lot more common sense than he did, especially under these pressure-cooker circumstances, now drew him aside. "You really have to get a handle on yourself," she urged. "If you keep this up, you'll scare all of the kitchen staff away. If they don't file a complaint against you for molestation first!"

"But someone is sabotaging my kitchen," he said. "Can't you see? Someone is out to get me." He darted a look at Marco, who was now regaling the others with his story of how he had eaten the pigeon poop, much to everyone's amusement. "And I have a pretty good idea who it is," he said, his jaw working furiously.

"Look, we'll deal with it, all right? The same way we always do. We'll get the plates back that haven't been touched yet, and those that have, we'll simply apologize and offer a free meal. But whatever you do, get a grip on yourself!"

Clearly, Kirsten was as upset as he was, only she wasn't upset about the bird poop but about his reaction. Which told him that she clearly had her priorities all wrong. Was he the only sane person in his whole restaurant? Somehow, he was starting to suspect that this just might be the case.

But then Ludo came hurrying back into the kitchen, carrying six plates. "No one has touched the stuff," he announced, and received an actual applause from his colleagues. "One person said he smelled it and thought it smelled funny so he didn't want to touch it, and another person said he thought it was seaweed and he doesn't like seaweed, and his wife said she thought it was just decoration and wasn't supposed to be eaten." He let out a sigh of relief. "So I think we're safe."

"Good job, Ludo," said Kirsten. "Now let's get these plates cleaned and start again. And if anyone knows who put this stuff on these plates, whether as a bad joke or whatever, please talk to me, all right? But not now. After the shift is over."

And as Roger resumed his position behind the stove, he

felt the eyes of his staff burning holes in his back. It looked like all of a sudden he was the bad guy.

Well, so be it. It was his restaurant, and he'd do whatever it took to save it, even if that meant that he'd ruin his own reputation and standing in the process.

He glanced over at Marco, who stood smiling to himself and shaking his head. Clearly, he thought the whole thing was extremely funny. Kirsten now joined him and exchanged a few words with the sous-chef, at which point they both turned their gaze on him, then quickly looked away again.

Just at that moment, Kirsten got a call on her cell and hurried out of the kitchen. "Have you found it?" he heard her ask. He didn't even want to know what that was about.

CHAPTER 27

Vesta and her small team of neighborhood watch members had been cruising the streets of Hampton Cove when she suddenly saw a curious sight: about two dozen cats were crowding on the sidewalk, and when she pulled the car over to take a look at what was going on, she recognized several of those cats.

"Why are we stopping again?" asked Wilbur. The shopkeeper's mood still hadn't improved.

"Cats," said Vesta curtly, and got out of the car.

When she got a little closer, she saw that it was, in fact, Kingman, and that for some reason he had surrounded himself with a large portion of the Hampton Cove cat population, among whom were her very own Harriet and Brutus.

"What's going on?" she asked. "What are you guys up to?"

"We're protecting Kingman," said Harriet. "He's under siege, and so we're acting as his bodyguards."

"While at the same time looking for Charlene," Brutus said.

"Not easy to pull off," said Kingman, who was darting nervous glances all over the place, his eyes moving like a pinball machine. "To look for a person while you're being hunted yourself. But we felt it was important to do something, so we gathered the Baker Street Cats—also known as cat choir—and have been cruising these streets looking for Charlene."

"That's very commendable," said Vesta. "But aren't you exaggerating a little? It doesn't really take a dozen cats to protect you, does it, Kingman?"

"But it does," he assured her. "You should have seen that madman. He had death in his eyes when he looked at me. And he was carrying a burlap sack."

"He really is a very dangerous man," Buster told her. "And we all care for Kingman, so we don't want any harm to come to him."

"Okay, get in the car," she said, pointing to her vehicle, which was idling on the curb.

"What?" said Kingman.

"You heard. We'll protect you for now. That way your friends are free to really look for Charlene, instead of having to stick to you like glue."

Kingman's face lit up like a Christmas tree. "You mean the watch is going to protect me?"

"Absolutely. From now on you're under the official protection of the neighborhood watch, and what more can you want for, huh? Hop in, big fella, and worry no more."

And so Kingman hopped into the car, quickly followed by Harriet and Brutus, who decided this was the perfect opportunity to take a load off their paws.

"As for the rest of you," said Vesta as she surveyed her feline troops. "Search high and low and leave no stone unturned until you have found Charlene, is that understood? She may be a human, but she's your mayor, too, all right?"

"Yes, Gran!" said the collected cats in unison and trotted

off to act as her emissaries in their search for the missing mayor.

She got back in the car, only to find that Wilbur was looking even more disgruntled than before.

"I thought I told you to stay put!" he was telling Kingman.

"I couldn't stay home, Wilbur," said Kingman. "Not with the mayor having been kidnapped. I'm Hampton Cove's feline mayor, you see, so it's my sacred duty to find and protect our human mayor."

"Cats," said Wilbur with disgust. "They never listen, do they?"

"On the contrary," said Vesta. "I find that they listen very well. It's you that doesn't listen," she told the irate shopkeeper. "Everyone strapped in?" she asked. And when only affirmative noises reached her from the backseat, she put the car in gear and they were off again.

They may not have found the mayor yet, but at least they had possibly saved Kingman's life and Harriet and Brutus's paws from overexertion.

"Look, all this aimless driving around isn't bringing us any closer to finding Charlene," said Wilbur. "We should approach this thing methodically, like the cops do. So we should ask ourselves who's got the most to gain by grabbing her."

They all thought about this for a moment. "I'd say that Uncle Alec has the most to gain," said Kingman. "After all, it often happens that men get tired of their wives a couple of weeks into the marriage. And so maybe he wanted to get rid of her and paid off a couple of crooks to put her on ice?"

She turned to the cat and gave him a look that immediately shut him up. As if her son could ever be capable of putting his own wife on ice. The gall of the cat! But since she didn't want to start an argument in front of Wilbur, she wisely kept her tongue.

"Charlene must have a lot of enemies," said Scarlett now, after having given the thing some thought. "I mean, she has been our mayor for quite a while now, and in her position she can't always give people what they want."

"What are you thinking?" Vesta asked.

"Well, maybe someone wanted to get married and she refused to issue a license because she felt they weren't compatible?"

"Mayors don't get involved in a couple's personal stuff," said Wilbur. "They issue their license and that's it. Though it's possible that a couple is trying to organize a fake marriage and in that case you might be right."

"Or maybe Charlene didn't want to give someone permission to build a house," Harriet suggested.

"Or to open a store in a certain location," Brutus said.

Vesta nodded. "I think we're onto something here. We should probably figure out who Charlene has upset at some point, and that might lead us to whoever grabbed her."

"Has anyone issued a ransom demand?" asked Scarlett.

"Not that I know of, and Alec promised he'd keep me informed."

Her phone had been suspiciously quiet for the past couple of hours, which told her that there hadn't been any new developments in the case.

"Okay, so if they haven't issued a ransom demand," said Wilbur, "that can only mean that they didn't take her for the money." His face clouded. "Which is probably bad news for us."

"And why is that?" asked Scarlett.

"Because that means this isn't a kidnapping. It's murder."

CHAPTER 28

After Sonny took off again in his van, we waited another ten minutes or so, just to be on the safe side. "You never know if he's waiting for us, Max," said Dooley, voicing my sentiments exactly. "And hoping to pounce when we least expect it."

"You're right, Dooley," I said. "Better safe than sorry."

But it was already getting dark, and frankly my tummy was rumbling and issuing me with a powerful reminder that it was probably time to go home.

We hadn't found Charlene yet, having accidentally climbed into the wrong van, but at least we knew that Sonny was involved in this whole sordid business somehow. And as we walked back in the direction of town, every time we saw a white van, we quickly hid behind a nearby bush, just to make sure Sonny couldn't carry out his threat of turning us into meatballs.

"Do you think people would eat a cat meatball?" asked Dooley.

"Only if they didn't know that it was a cat meatball," I

assured him. "Once they know they're eating their pet, I don't think it will taste as good anymore."

"But humans eat everything, Max," said Dooley. "I saw this documentary the other day on the Discovery Channel about this guy who wanted to taste every single animal on the face of the planet before he died. And so he ate elephants, giraffes, gnus, kangaroos, moles. He even ate a bluebottle fly once." He shivered. "Can you imagine?"

"That man must have been either deranged or very, very bored," I said.

"And also very, very rich to afford to buy all of those animals and pay a cook to prepare them. Even if Odelia wanted to eat an elephant, I think she'd find it hard to do so. It's not as if they sell elephant meat at the local deli."

And a good thing, too. We were finally on familiar terrain again, and as traffic increased in intensity, I knew we were close to home. And as we crossed the road, suddenly a car screeched to a halt not five inches from us. Oops!

The door opened and a familiar voice cried out, "Are you crazy! I could have hit you!"

It was Gran. "Oh, Gran, I'm so happy to see you!" said Dooley.

"What were you thinking!" the old lady bellowed, sounding extremely upset. She had a point, of course. We hadn't been thinking. We had been talking about crazy people tasting exotic animals and eating bluebottle flies.

And so we hopped into the car and saw that we were joining a pretty diverse company: Harriet was there, and also Brutus and Kingman, and Wilbur and Scarlett. "What are you guys up to?" I asked as I wedged myself in between Kingman and Brutus, which wasn't an easy feat to accomplish since space is definitely at a premium in Gran's little red Peugeot.

"We're assisting the watch in trying to locate Charlene," said Kingman. "And since Gran felt it was advisable to make sure I was safe from the tentacles of this maniac Sonny, she was kind enough to put me under her personal protection."

"Pretty soon she'll offer you a safe house, too," said Brutus with a grin.

Gran slammed the door, still looking discombobulated. "Imagine almost driving over my own cats," she muttered. "I'd never forgive myself."

"Good thing you have super-fast reflexes," said Scarlett.

"Oh, I'm an excellent driver," said Gran as she stomped on the accelerator and the car sort of jerked forward, like a bucking stallion trying to get rid of a pesky rider. We were all thrown back against the seat, and for a moment, no one spoke while we all counted our limbs to see if they were still attached.

"Wilbur thinks that Charlene is probably dead already," Kingman said. "What do you think?"

"Oh, she's not dead at all," I said. "We just saw Johnny Carew pick up a spaghetti meal to bring to Charlene because she didn't like the food that he and Jerry gave her. So if she's still taking nourishment, she probably isn't dead. I mean, dead people don't eat, right?"

They all stared at me, and none more than Gran, with the benefit of the rear-view mirror. Her car might be old, but it has all the amenities of modern automobiles. Her eyes were penetrating and inquisitive, and so I trudged on and told the select gathering all about our recent adventures and findings. Before long, they were hanging on my lips, which was very gratifying, I found, and beneficial for my ego, which may not be large but still likes it when it gets all the attention. Which is when Gran jerked the wheel sideways in a sudden impulse, performed a brusque U-turn, and almost plowed into an oncoming Mercedes, whose driver had to stomp on the brakes to avoid a full-on collision. In spite of all this, the driver still found the time to lean on his horn, open the window, and yell an expletive.

"Where are you going?" asked Scarlett after she had recovered from the shock. Contrary to Gran, she hadn't understood a word I said, so she was behind in the narrative, as was Wilbur. But then Gran told her fellow watch members that she'd suddenly had this hunch or instinct that told her to head in the opposite direction than the one she'd been traveling in.

"Gut instinct," she said. "Call it a feeling or presentiment, but I think I know where we might be able to find Charlene."

"Oh, my God," said Wilbur, raising his eyes heavenward. "And now all of a sudden, she's psychic!"

Following my instructions, Gran directed her car to the address where Sonny lived, and sure enough, we found his van parked in front of the building.

"He's here," I told her.

"Which means we better pay him a visit," she said, a resolute look stealing over her. I knew what that meant. Sonny was in big trouble!

"Do you mind if we stay in the car, Gran?" asked Dooley. "Sonny doesn't like cats. He said he wants to turn us into meatballs and serve us to his daughter and her boyfriend."

Gran's face worked as she processed these words. "You're coming," she said. "And if that man so much as looks at you funny, I'll turn *him* into a meatball!"

CHAPTER 29

Charlene tapped the tabletop nervously while gazing out of the window at the landscape that stretched out before her eyes. She knew exactly where she was, of course. The old Fraser Bailey farm on Helms Road. Vale and Carew might be a lot of things, but they weren't exactly original thinkers, as the farm had been the location they had used in a previous incarnation to keep the cats of Hampton Cove they had kidnapped. That endeavor hadn't lasted long, and the cats had all been returned home safely. And so she wasn't too worried about her own fate.

The thing was that she had a lot of stuff on her desk, and every moment she spent locked up in this silly vaudeville was time she could have spent clearing her desk. She thought of Alec, who would be frantic with worry, and her staff at Town Hall, who would be beside themselves with concern. And all the while she sat there, languishing, caught by the two worst crooks in the business. It was an insult. A disgrace. But mostly it was all extremely pointless and unnecessary.

And so when the key turned in the lock and the door opened, she was ready to tell Johnny exactly how she felt about this nonsense. But instead, she found that his partner in crime, Jerry Vale, had entered, wearing that same silly mask Johnny had been wearing.

"Now what is it?" she asked, unable to hide her irritation.

"The spaghetti is on its way, Madam Mayor," said Jerry with the right amount of obsequiousness. "So I was wondering, what would you like with that? A soda? Beer? Wine? We could offer you a choice of a tasty red or a very crisp white."

"Oh, who cares about any of that," she burst out, causing the other man to blink. "When are you finally going to end this farce and let me go? Unlike some people I won't mention, I actually have a job, you know, a job I should get back to."

"I have a job," said Jerry defensively.

"Oh? So you call this a job, do you? Kidnapping people for money?"

"Oh, but this isn't about money, Madam Mayor," he said. "This is about righting a wrong. And I, for one, feel very sympathetic with your ex-husband, since I went through exactly this same ordeal myself. When Marlene announced that she wanted a divorce—"

"My ex-husband? What are you talking about?"

"I probably shouldn't tell you this, but I'll say this much: your ex-husband was very sad when you divorced him, and so he wants to ask you to give him a second chance. And since he knows you probably won't listen to him, he decided to put you in a position where you would be forced to, if you see what I mean."

She stared at them. "Jerry Vale, if you don't stop babbling and start making sense, I'm going to throw this fork at you."

Jerry uttered a squeak of shock at the mention of his name. "But..."

"Yes, yes. Of course I know who you are. You and Carew. But you were talking about my ex-husband?"

"Well, yes. I don't think I'm betraying any confidences when I tell you that that man still loves you very much and in fact has never stopped loving you and would like you to give him a second chance. Now I know that you're married to Chief Lip, but he feels that's just a rebound thing and if you will simply hear him out…"

"Look, obviously you've been had, Vale," she said, not unkindly, for she knew these weren't exactly top criminals she was dealing with. "Jim died years ago, so whoever hired you to do this, it wasn't him. Unless he rose from the grave."

Vale looked stunned by this piece of news. "But-but-but…"

"Okay, so why don't we make a deal? You let me go right now, and in return I won't make life too difficult for you." She couldn't let them off the hook, but at least she could work with Alec and the judge to give them some kind of lighter sentence. After all, they had gone out of their way to cook her a decent meal.

"But-but-but…"

Just then, the front door of the old farmhouse slammed open and a voice caroled, "I've got the spaghetti! Do you want to have a taste first, Jer?"

"In here, Johnny!" Jerry yelled.

Johnny carefully stepped into the room and must have become aware that the scene was a little tense, for he said, "Everything all right?"

"Madam Mayor just told me that her ex-husband is dead," said Jerry. "Dead, Johnny! Which means we've been had! Taken for a couple of fools!"

"But he can't be dead," said Johnny. "He asked us to make sure to set the scene for a romantic dinner." He gave Charlene a fervent look. "I even bought candles and got you that music that you like so much, Madam Mayor."

"And what music would that be?" asked Charlene, who had gone back to tapping her fingers on the table.

"Why, Bolero, of course. He said it was the music that played on your first date."

"As far as I remember—and I've tried very hard to forget everything connected with that awful man—the music that played on our first date was Tony Bennett, not Bolero. So whoever has been feeding you this cock-and-bull story obviously doesn't know the first thing about me or my life married to Jim Hobbin. And now if you will please let me get on with my business. This has frankly taken enough time already, wouldn't you say? Wasting my time and yours?"

Johnny and Jerry shared a look as Jerry slowly took off his mask. "She knows who we are, Johnny," said the smaller of the two crooks as his ferret-like face appeared. He looked absolutely crestfallen, and whether it was because the happy romantic ending he had envisioned wasn't in the cards or because the gig was up was hard to determine—maybe it was both.

"Yeah, I know," said Johnny. "I didn't want to tell you, but she was on to us from the start."

Jerry sighed. "That's what you get when you become famous. Very hard to keep doing your job."

"It's true. The same thing happens to spies, you know. After a while all the bad guys know who James Bond is, and they can see him coming from miles away."

Charlene actually started feeling sorry for the two goons, and said, "So what's all this I hear about your spaghetti? Is it really as good as advertised?"

Johnny's face lit up with a smile. "Oh, it's the best. Sonny —that's Jerry's ex-brother-in-law Sonny Hayworth—isn't a great chef, but he does whip up a pretty decent spaghetti. Isn't that right, Jer?"

Jerry was giving his partner the evil eye and now slapped his beefy arm.

"Ouch! Why did you hit me!"

"You just went and told her Sonny's name, you idiot!"

Johnny grinned. "I guess I did, didn't I? Oh well, it doesn't matter. Sonny's got nothing to do with this. Except that he cooked her his famous spaghetti. It's the meatballs that are a real treat," he added for Charlene's benefit. "He makes them himself, and I don't know what he puts into them, but they're to die for."

And since she was actually pretty hungry, Charlene suggested they share Sonny's famous meatballs and spaghetti, and since the table in her makeshift prison was a little too small for three, they moved into the kitchen and enjoyed their meal there. And it had to be said, whatever else his qualities might or might not be, Sonny's meatballs were indeed to die for.

"He claims he puts a secret ingredient in them," said Johnny as he chewed down with relish. "And he refuses to tell us what it is. But I think it's pork."

"It's not pork," said Jerry. "It's lamb."

"Whatever it is," said Charlene "it's pretty tasty. So this Sonny character is your brother-in-law, huh, Jerry?"

"He was. Before Marlene divorced me," said Jerry sadly. "And now Valerie is divorcing Sonny. Kicked him out of the house and Kiki—that's their daughter—spends every other weekend with her dad and the rest of the time lives with Val."

"She has a boyfriend, though, doesn't she, Jer?" said Johnny, who was relishing his meal and wasn't afraid to let it be known by smacking his lips with relish.

"Supposedly. No idea if it's true or not. Sonny asked Kiki, but she refuses to tell."

"Clever girl," said Charlene. "She probably doesn't want

to be put in a tough spot. Having to spy on her mom for her dad and vice versa. That's the worst."

"So who's the guy?" asked Johnny.

"Like I said, I have no idea if there even is a guy," said Jerry. "Though to be honest it wouldn't surprise me. After she kicked out Sonny, she said that the next guy she'd marry wouldn't be a crook." His face sagged. "Marlene said the same thing when she divorced me."

"And is she?" asked Charlene. "Dating someone who's not a crook?"

Jerry shrugged. "If she is, she's not telling me."

"She wasn't happy that Jerry couldn't bring in the big bucks," said Johnny as he leaned forward and took on a conspiratorial tone. "Isn't that so, Jer?"

"Yeah, she felt she was wasting her time with a small-time operator like me. Said she wanted me to join the big leagues, or else she was out. She was big on jewelry and fancy clothes, Marlene was, and when I couldn't get her what she wanted, she bailed on me." He sighed. "Maybe she was right. I am a small-time operator. I mean, look at us, Johnny. We can't even do a decent kidnapping."

"I think we did do a decent kidnapping," said Johnny. "We can't help it that the guy ordering the kidnapping wasn't on the level."

"So how was it that someone ordered my kidnapping?" asked Charlene.

"No idea," said Johnny. "We only spoke on the phone. Isn't that right, Jer?"

"Yeah, and he was using one of those voice-changing thingies, so we wouldn't recognize his voice."

"So it was definitely a man?" asked Charlene.

"Could have been a woman. Like I said, they changed their voice. Though I figured it was your ex-husband. But if you're telling us he's dead, that's us being taken for fools, isn't it?"

"Oh, don't be too hard on yourself, Jer," said Johnny. "We got to spend a nice time with Madam Mayor here and enjoy a great meal together. How often do you get the chance to rub shoulders with a famous politician like her, huh?"

Charlene had to suppress a smile. Famous politician—yeah, right. She wiped her lips. "This was delicious. So now what? Are you going to let me go or what?"

Jerry shrugged and shared a look with Johnny. "I guess," he said. "Though whoever hired us to kidnap you probably won't be happy."

"It could be an ex-boyfriend," Johnny suggested. "The one that got away?"

"Nobody got away," she said resolutely. "I'm a happily married woman and there is absolutely no one in my past that I ever want to spend another minute with. So whoever hired you, it definitely was no ex-boyfriend, since they're all married to other people by now."

Johnny held up his hands. "I guess it will have to remain a mystery."

Until Alec worked it out, Charlene thought. "So? Can I go home now?"

Jerry nodded. "Yeah, let's call it quits. We've all been had, and if I ever get my hands on this person, I'll wring their neck for making us look like idiots."

Something told her that these two didn't need anybody else to do that, but she wasn't going to risk angering them—just in case they changed their minds.

But the meatballs had worked their magic, and both crooks were in a good mood as they downed utensils and escorted her to their van. Moments later they were on their way into town, and it looked as if Charlene's harrowing adventure was at an end.

CHAPTER 30

*A*lec Lip was beside himself with worry, but even more than the constant worry about Charlene's fate was the notion that there wasn't a whole lot he could do. The entire police force was on the case, with its officers out on the streets en masse, talking to people, looking for possible clues, and generally doing whatever they could to find the mayor. He would have been out there with them, but Chase and Odelia had determined that it was best if he stayed put and manned the phones with them to collect every snippet of information they could gather.

And so he sat in the main office with his niece and her husband while they collated all the facts that hopefully would, at some point, lead to a breakthrough. So far they had determined that Charlene's kidnapping had probably been made to order, and that the people who had actually taken her were simply hired muscle. They had excellent footage of the moment she was taken, and even though the men wore masks, it was clear Vale and Carew were the culprits.

They had been able to follow the van as it drove out of town, but then unfortunately no more CCTV or traffic cameras had been available to track their further progress, almost as if they knew where to go without being seen. All they knew was that they had left town in a northeastern direction, traveling along country roads, but that still left a vast area to cover where she could be held. If they hadn't left the area entirely and had kept on going in the direction of neighboring towns.

Still, hope springs eternal, and so they had redirected their efforts to that part of the greater Hampton Cove territory in the hopes of stumbling upon some derelict farmhouse or maybe a witness who had seen some suspicious activity.

He checked the big clock over the door of the main office. Eight o'clock and still nothing. He'd drunk liters of coffee and hadn't really eaten anything decent for hours, but even if he wanted to, he couldn't get a bite down his throat. Not as long as his wife was out there. He knew that Vale and Carew might be crooks, but they weren't actually violent men. Still, the person they had kidnapped Charlene for could be some maniac who felt wronged by something she did in her capacity as mayor at some point. He could be a psychopath who might inflict untold harm on the woman he loved. His nerves were wrecked, and so was he.

"Don't worry, boss," said Chase, who could see he was suffering. "We'll find her."

"Oh, I don't doubt that we will," he said. "The question is, how will we find her?"

"Alive and well," Odelia stressed.

Dolores, the station dispatcher, who had also joined them in the main office room, now put down the phone and said in her croaky voice, "That was Kurt Mayfield. He says your mother kidnapped his dog Fifi this afternoon without his permission and he wants to file a complaint."

He waved an impatient hand. "Later," he said gruffly. Who

cared about what his mother was up to? She had promised him that she would get Charlene home safe and sound, but to be honest, he just wished she would stay out of this altogether.

"The coroner's report came back on Alan Gerard," said Chase as he read something on his computer screen. "He died from cardiac arrest. No signs of a struggle or any signs of any bodily harm inflicted on him. Looks like the stress of being tied to that chair and his house ransacked was too much for him. He did have a heart condition." He leaned back. "I also contacted his next of kin and they told me that in his later years, Mr. Gerard had become increasingly solitary, effectively becoming something of a recluse and wouldn't talk to anyone."

"Later," said Alec irritably. Who cared about any of that now?

His sister walked into the office carrying a steaming plate of something that might be food. "Here," she said, putting the plate in front of his nose.

He waved her away.

"But Alec, you have to eat something," she insisted.

"How can I eat when Charlene is out there?" he said. "It's impossible."

But Marge insisted and pointed to the plate. "Eat," she said.

And so he picked up the fork she handed him and tried to put some of it into his mouth. It actually tasted pretty good. He glanced up when Tex approached. The doctor gave him a look of concern. "I don't like the way you look, Alec."

"I don't care," he said gruffly.

"Tex is right," said Marge. "Your skin tone—it's almost gray."

"I don't care about my skin tone!" he exclaimed.

His sister and her husband distanced themselves for a moment and carried on a whispered conversation.

"Could be his heart," Tex murmured.

"Maybe you should check his pulse," Marge suggested.

"He won't let me," Tex responded. "He's being very stubborn."

"Then I'll do it," Marge suggested. "I'm his sister, he won't refuse."

They both approached again, and he saw Tex was carrying his doctor's bag.

"Look, I'm fine!" he said. "But as long as Charlene isn't found, I'm not interested in what any of you have to say. I don't care about food, or the Alan Gerards of this world, or what happened to Kurt's dog, or how bad I look, all right? So let's just focus on finding Charlene. Time is of the essence, people."

And didn't he know it. If a kidnapping victim isn't found within the first twenty-four hours, chances are they might never be found, or at least not alive.

Tex now pressed a finger to the Chief's wrist and stared at his watch for a moment. Then he took out his gadget to gauge Alec's blood pressure and wrapped it tightly around his arm. "I'm sorry, but I don't like your color," he insisted.

And he was just about to swat him away like a pesky fly when Jerry Vale walked in, followed by Johnny Carew, followed by… Charlene!

For a moment, he thought he was seeing things. That he had fallen asleep at his desk and was dreaming. But then Charlene gave him a dazzling smile and he realized it wasn't a dream but very much real. And as he clasped her in his arms, he actually started sobbing like a little baby.

CHAPTER 31

Sonny didn't like cats. He had never liked cats. Not when he was a boy and one had scratched him when he was just trying to be nice. Not when he was a teenager and his girlfriend had planted a cat on his lap, telling him it was the ultimate relationship test. He had recoiled in horror, and she had immediately broken up with him. And not when he was still married to Valerie and Kiki had insisted on getting a cat as a pet. Despite his protestations, Val had made him run down to the pet store and get their daughter one of those horrible creatures.

Of course, the cat had soon become the ruler of their household, always singling him out by crawling onto his lap, making him sit there frozen in fear of being ripped to shreds. Or making him spend a fortune on kibble and litter and whatever else those creatures needed. So when Kingman had squealed on him at the General Store, it was par for the course, and he knew it was only to be expected.

But the last thing he thought he'd see was three pensioners standing on his doorstep with no fewer than five of those monstrous creatures in tow! He wanted to shut the door in their faces, but one of the old fogies, a crusty-looking dame who reminded him of Estelle Getty for some reason, had already planted a treacherous foot in the gap and forced her way in, those cats following behind.

"What the hell!" he cried at this home invasion. "What's the big idea?"

In the living room, Kiki, who had been watching something on television, watched the scene with interest, which was a first. "What's going on, Dad?" she asked. "Who are all these people?"

"How the hell should I know?!" he exclaimed. But then he recognized that big cat belonging to Wilbur Vickery—and of course, the man himself. "Oh, I see," he said. "This is about me stealing that spaghetti, is it? I thought you said you'd let it go, man! You promised!"

"This isn't about that," said Wilbur, who didn't look entirely happy to be there. "This is about Charlene Butterwick being kidnapped and you being involved with the kidnappers."

"Johnny Carew and Jerry Vale?" said the crusty dame, narrowing her eyes at him. "Ring a bell, Sonny Jim?"

He sternly shook his head. "Never heard of them," he said.

"Jerry Vale is my uncle," said Kiki, the treacherous child. "What has he gone and done now?"

"He kidnapped the mayor of this town," said Scarlett as she took a seat next to the teenager. "So he's your uncle, is he?"

"Well, kinda," said Kiki. "He used to be married to my aunt Marlene, so I guess that makes him my ex-uncle or something?"

"He's still your uncle!" Sonny insisted. "That divorce was a sham, and Marlene and Jerry will get back together again. True love always prevails!"

"Of course, Dad," said Kiki with the perfect eye roll. "Whatever you say."

"Look, whatever my brother-in-law is up to, it's got nothing to do with me," said Sonny.

"Then why was Johnny in here just now?" asked the old lady, who seemed to be very well informed. Too well informed for his liking! "Picking up spaghetti for Charlene? Huh? Tell me that!" she said, poking his chest with a bony finger.

"Dad, did you give my spaghetti to the mayor?" asked Kiki. She turned to the old lady. "I didn't want it, but my mom made me come back to eat it. But then I told Dad that if he wanted me to tell Mom that I had eaten it all, I'd do it, but only if he promised to raise my allowance." She settled back. "I hate that spaghetti."

"You used to love my spaghetti!" said Sonny. "Nobody makes spaghetti sauce like your mostest favorite daddy in the whole wide world!"

"Oh, Dad," said Kiki with the sigh of a long-suffering teenager. "Your spaghetti isn't bad, but it's not as good as…"

He turned on her. "Not as good as whose? Just say it!"

"Not as good as Mom's new boyfriend's spaghetti, all right? He's an actual pro."

Her words were like a knife to the heart. "That's impossible. My spaghetti is the best."

She shrugged. "If you say so."

"Okay, so spill, buddy," said the old lady. "Where are they holding the mayor? And why did they take her? Who are they working for?"

"And where did you stash the loot?" asked Wilbur.

He looked from one of his nemeses to the next. "Loot? What loot!"

"Vesta, tell him about the loot," said Wilbur, turning to the crusty dame.

"You were seen entering the home belonging to Alan Gerard and stealing a package containing a painting from the attic," said Vesta. He vaguely seemed to remember that Chief Lip's mother was called Vesta. Could this be her? If so, he was in some real trouble here. "So what did you do with that painting, huh?"

He stared at her. "How do you know!" he cried, before realizing he probably should have kept his mouth shut.

"I know a lot of things," she said. "Now start talking!"

"Dad, have you been up to bad things again?" asked Kiki. "Mom won't be happy, you know. You promised you were done with all of that."

And so he broke down. He could lie to these people, but he couldn't lie to his daughter. "Okay, I admit it! I stole that painting. But it wasn't for me. They told me to get it, so I did, all right?"

"Who told you to steal it?" asked Vesta. "Was it the same people who told your brother-in-law to kidnap the mayor and to attack Alan Gerard this morning?"

"I don't know anything about that," he said. "I had nothing to do with the death of that old man. But yeah, it's probably the same people, since they first asked me to babysit the mayor, but I told them that I wasn't doing it. Kiki is right. I did make a promise I was done with all of that, and so I said no."

"And yet I caught you stealing those spaghetti ingredients," said Wilbur.

"Dad!" said Kiki, her face expressing surprise. "You *stole* that spaghetti?"

"I did not steal any spaghetti!" said Sonny. He had had it up to here with people making all kinds of accusations against him. "I only stole the ingredients to make the best spaghetti sauce in the world: *my* spaghetti sauce." But then Kiki gave him a look of such disappointment, he relented.

"Do you know how much that stuff costs these days? Inflation is a dirty trick bankers and politicians play on the working class, honey, and I'm not playing their game anymore."

"So you steal from a hardworking local business owner instead," said Wilbur. "You are a real piece of work, aren't you, Sonny?"

"Where is that painting now?" asked Vesta, keeping her eye on the ball.

"I don't have it anymore," he said. "I left it at the arranged drop-off point and, in return, got my finder's fee."

"So who told you to steal it?"

"No idea."

"You're lying, Sonny."

"I swear I'm not! They had one of those voice-changing apps on their phone or something. I couldn't even tell if it was a man or a woman. All I know is they told me to find that painting and then drop it off at the park. So I put it in one of the trash cans on the side of the park and fished an envelope out of that same trash can with the money. I've never seen these people, and I doubt if I ever will."

"Ask my uncle Jerry," said Kiki. "He'll know. He's a crook, same as Dad, only he gets things done."

"You shouldn't listen to your mother," he said, but couldn't hide how much her words stung. First the spaghetti and now this? "At least I didn't kidnap the mayor! How dumb is that, huh? Like trying to kidnap the President."

"Sonny Hayworth," said Vesta. "I'm making a citizen's arrest. Please come with us to the police station. If you come quietly, I won't have to use violence."

He laughed. "You and whose army, toots! Now get lost, will you? All of you, and take those filthy rats along with you, before I turn them into meatballs!"

But then suddenly Vesta took out a can of pepper spray and actually maced him! It stung, but what stung more than the mace was the fact that Kiki had to see that. It probably wouldn't win him any points in the Parent of the Year competition.

CHAPTER 32

I thought Gran would drive Mr. Hayworth back to the police station personally, and I wasn't exactly looking forward to riding in the same car as the man who wanted to turn us all into meatballs. But wiser counsels prevailed, and instead she called her son and told him to send a couple of officers to take Sonny to the station. And while she was on the phone with Uncle Alec, he informed her the search was over, and that Charlene had been returned to him safe and sound.

"How did that happen?" asked Scarlett once we were back in the car.

The police officers had dropped by and had arrested Sonny, for real this time, and taken him away. Kiki had decided to go home to her mother, and so it looked like our adventure was over, which I was extremely happy about, to be honest.

"She just walked into the police station," said Gran.

"They let her go?" asked Wilbur.

"They did. She had a good talk with her kidnappers, they

shared a nice meal together, and then they decided they might as well drive her back to town."

"I don't get it," said Wilbur. "She had a meal with her kidnappers and a nice long talk?"

"That seems to be about the gist of it," said Gran. "Turns out Vale and Carew thought they were doing all this for her ex-husband, who claimed to still be in love with her and wanting her back. So when she told them that her ex-husband died a couple of years ago, they realized they'd been taken for fools, and so they turned themselves in."

"Well, I'll be..." said Wilbur, scratching his scalp. "And who hired them if it wasn't her ex-husband?"

"No idea. Though it could be the same person who hired Sonny. Whoever it was also used a voice-changing app when he called to give them their instructions. And he seemed to know an awful lot about Charlene, since he told them where to find her."

"That probably wasn't hard," said Scarlett. "Everyone knows where Charlene's office is, and that she works long hours."

"Yeah, I guess so," said Gran. "But if this really was the same person, how did they know about Alan Gerard's painting, which probably must be worth a lot of money if they took it? He probably didn't tell the whole world about that."

"No, probably not," Scarlett admitted. She leaned back. "Anyway, I'm so glad this ordeal is over. Did they at least treat her well?"

"Looks like it," said Gran. "They definitely tried their darndest to give her the kind of food she likes, and even got her the kind of spaghetti she loves."

Dooley turned to me. "I really hope Sonny didn't put actual cat meat in his meatballs, Max. Or else Charlene may have just eaten a cat."

We all shivered at his words. "They should have that meat

examined," said Brutus. "And if it does contain cat, they should throw the book at this man for catricide, a crime I feel should probably be on par with homicide."

"I can't believe anyone could be so cruel," said Harriet. "But then he did look like a very cruel and mean man. Even his own daughter doesn't seem to like him all that much." She sighed. "Okay, so now that's over and done with, let's get back to the real issue of the day. Have you guys decided yet?"

"Decided what?" I asked, still thinking about Sonny and his association with Johnny and Jerry.

"If you're going to be my assistants or not. I was thinking three should be fine. Brutus could be my warm-up act. You know, like in talk shows there's always a person who entertains the live studio audience and gets them in the mood and tells them when to laugh and when to applaud? You could do the same for me. And then Max could make sure everyone knows their parts. Really drill them, you know. And Dooley..." She paused as she studied our friend. "Well, I guess you could be cat choir's mascot. Every sports team has a mascot, after all, so I guess we should also have one. And you would fit the bill perfectly."

Dooley seemed extraordinarily happy with this. "Ooh, thank you so much, Harriet. I would love to be cat choir's mascot. So what do I have to do, exactly?"

"Um, just stand there and look happy, you know," said Harriet. "And don't talk too much. As a rule, mascots don't talk."

"I can do that," said Dooley. "Where do you want me to stand?"

"Off to the side, so you don't stick out too much," she advised. "Mascots are fine, but they're no substitute for the star of the show, which is me." She thrust out her chest. "So the way I see it is that Brutus warms up the crowd, Max makes sure they all know what to do and take their positions,

Dooley makes them feel warm and fuzzy, and connected as a team, and then I arrive to loud cheers and feed on the energy of the audience." She sighed happily as she clasped her paws together. "This is going to be so great, you guys. Like a dress rehearsal for the bigger and much larger audience I'm sure will be my destiny further down the line."

"Cat choir isn't exactly our audience, though, is it?" I said. "They're a choir, so you will have to work with them, not expect them to applaud after your performance."

"I know that," she said haughtily. "Don't you think I know that? But every star has to start somewhere, and I might as well start here, with cat choir, the first witnesses to the star that is about to be born." She pressed a paw to her chest. "Moi," she said, throwing her head back.

We had arrived at the police station just in time to see Sonny being escorted in, hands cuffed and a sort of dejected look on his face. It looked like he wouldn't get to make his favorite spaghetti sauce for a while. Unless of course they assigned him to the prison kitchen and he could demonstrate his cooking skills there.

We walked in to find Charlene and Uncle Alec at the center of attention. Even though it was getting late, all of the police officers who had been instrumental in scouring the streets of our town for the missing mayor were in there and gave a loud and hearty cheer as Charlene finished up her impromptu speech to the troops, thanking them all for their efforts and going to the limit to end her ordeal.

"You're what makes me proud to be a Hampton Covian," she said. "And if it wasn't for you, the likes of Vale and Carew and Hayworth would still be out there, creating trouble for people. So from the bottom of my heart, thank you!"

A loud applause rang out, and I could see that everyone was extremely relieved that the mayor's ordeal had been so short-lived. No one was happier than Uncle Alec, though, who actually had tears in his eyes as he stood next to his wife. The poor guy had clearly suffered—I even had the impression he had lost a few pounds over the course of a single day.

The group dispersed, and everyone went back to their regular business, which in most cases was going home after a long and stressful day. We joined our humans, who all stood crowded around Uncle Alec's desk. And as Vesta relayed the story of how she had made a citizen's arrest, the question on everyone's lips was who this mystery person could be who was at the heart of the whole thing. Chase vowed he wouldn't rest until he had this mastermind behind bars, but since they were all tired, they decided to go home and take another crack at it tomorrow.

Which is when Marge suggested they all go out for a bite to eat. Since none of them had had dinner—except apparently Charlene—that idea was immediately embraced with general excitement. And so we soon found ourselves outside again, and since the restaurant they had picked wasn't far, they decided to walk. Wilbur wasn't joining us, since he was eager to get home and have an early night's sleep and then open up his beloved General Store again early in the morning.

So we said goodbye to Kingman for now and joined our humans.

"I just hope they don't serve meatballs," said Brutus.

And I think we all agreed with that sentiment.

CHAPTER 33

The Hungry Pipe happens to be Harriet and Brutus's favorite restaurant since it has the benefit of a rooftop terrace that's very popular with locals and tourists alike. Once the restaurant closes shop for the night, it puts its leftovers to the side to be taken down for trash collection in the morning. Many a night, Harriet and Brutus have spent a romantic time on that roof, gazing out at a full moon while snacking on some of the most exquisite food known to cat-kind.

The restaurant itself had recently changed ownership, with a hot and dynamic young chef taking the reins and revitalizing the place to the extent that it was now packed with diners every single night. It was hard to secure a table if you didn't book weeks in advance or were a VIP or celebrity. In other words, the Hungry Pipe had suddenly become the 'it' place. But since Charlene is the mayor and she had recently gone through a horrific ordeal, which had been widely reported on, the moment we set foot in the place, every single person in there looked up in surprise and then began applauding to show their support and celebrate her safe return from capture. And so before long, they added an extra table and our company was invited to have dinner on the house.

The restaurant's owner, one Kirsten Turton, personally dropped by for a chat and to express her heartfelt sympathy to Charlene and to tell her how they had all been extremely worried about her. Even Chef Roger Turton stepped out of his kitchen for a moment to greet us and express his delight at Charlene's return.

Moments later, we were all looking at the menu, though when I say 'we,' I mean 'them,' since cats don't really pick food off the menu. Then again, whatever they decided to give us was fine by me since I was starving after having been on my paws all day.

So when Brutus said, "Let's go," with a sort of gleam in his eyes, I merely stared at him in surprise and dismay.

"But I want to eat," I said, not beating about the bush.

"And you will, but not here," said Brutus.

"Trust Brutus to find the best food in the house," said Harriet with a smile, and trotted off after her mate. And since I was intrigued in spite of myself, I decided to follow them.

"Max, wait up!" said Dooley, hurrying along in our wake.

Moments later, Brutus was mounting a staircase that led to the roof, and we followed behind him. "Trust me," he said. "You won't be disappointed."

I certainly hoped not, since my stomach was practically stuck to my ribs at that point. If this went on for much longer, I wouldn't have the strength to go on!

We arrived on the roof, and I saw that plenty more people were gathered there. Another chef stood whipping up food on a grill, while another did something that involved flames rising from a pan, and the diners looking on cried out in delight. It looked more like a show than a dinner, but then I guess it's all part of the experience of eating at a fancy place like the Hungry Pipe.

"Over here!" Brutus yelled as we looked around to see where he could have gone. We found him behind a small structure that had been erected on the roof, and I finally saw what he had been referring to. Here, the servers deposited the plates the diners had finished—or, as it turned out, in most cases, hadn't finished.

It is a truth most universally acknowledged that a single cat in possession of a good appetite must be in want of a meal, and so before long, we all dug in with relish. And I had to admit that Brutus hadn't been lying: this stuff was delish!

"Why do people leave so much food on their plates, Max?" asked Dooley between two bites.

"No idea, Dooley," I said. "Maybe they weren't as hungry as they thought they were? Or maybe they didn't like the taste once their food arrived?"

It was true what he said, though. Most of the plates were still half-full, and in some cases, people had only taken a nibble before pushing the plate aside and deciding to forgo eating the rest. Not that I was complaining, for it offered us a nice sampling of all the different dishes on the menu. Like a smorgasbord of taste. Gordon Ramsay may not have approved, but it certainly got my vote.

Suddenly, as we were thusly engaged, I caught sight of movement from the corner of my eye, and when I looked up —with some reluctance since I wasn't fully satisfied yet—I saw that we had been joined by none other than our good friend Clarice!

"Hey, Clarice," said Dooley. "So great to see you!"

"Hey, Dooley," said Clarice with a half-grin. "I see you have discovered Hampton Cove's best-kept secret, huh?"

"Oh, we've been coming here for years," said Harriet. "Though it has been a while, hasn't it, sparky star?"

"Been busy," said Brutus between two bites. "Saving mayors and such."

"Oh, I heard about that," said Clarice as she also jumped up onto the table and sniffed around for something that was to her liking. "So did you find her?"

"Yeah, we did," I said. "Well, not we, exactly. Charlene managed to save herself by talking her kidnappers out of the idea."

"Now ain't that something?" Clarice mused as she set her sights on a plate that was still full to bursting and dug in with relish.

Clarice is a formerly feral cat who had recently been adopted by Scarlett Canyon, but even though she now enjoyed the comforts of having a home, she still liked to keep up with some of her old habits, like roaming these restaurants for leftovers. "Ever since they got this new chef, this place is rocking," she revealed. "Gourmet food all around. The guy knows his business, that's for sure."

"That would be Roger Turton, right?" I said. "We saw him downstairs."

"Oh, so you met the chef, did you? I also met him once, and I have to say it was not an experience I'm likely to forget."

"And why is that?" I asked.

She shrugged. "He may love to cook for humans, but he clearly doesn't like it when we touch it."

"He doesn't like cats, is that it?"

"It's not that he doesn't like us. It's more that he's afraid of his restaurant's reputation when the regular diners see us eating from their plates. It's below the kind of standard he wants to set. And I have to say he's got a point. Most people going out for dinner don't enjoy the spectacle of a member of another species eating from their plates, whether they be mice or rats or cats."

"You can't really put us on a par with rats, Clarice," said Harriet. "Cats are distinguished, classy, gracious animals. Whereas rats are… well, rats!"

"All I'm saying is to make sure Chef Turton doesn't see you," said Clarice. "For if he does, he's likely to come after you with a broom and chase you away. He might even personally throw you off this roof. He's that fussy about the place."

We all looked up, but when we didn't see any sign of the restaurant owner anywhere nearby, we settled down again. But then all of a sudden a loud voice called out, "Hey! Will you get away from there!" And suddenly a man was upon us, trying to actually swat us with the back of his hand! And so we all skedaddled, making sure he wouldn't throw us off the roof!

Once we were away from this person, hiding nearby, Clarice said, "That's Ludo. He's not a bad sort, but if he doesn't get rid of us, his boss will give him hell. Anyway, he'll be gone soon, and then we can go back."

"Are you crazy!" said Harriet. "I'm not going back there."

"Suit yourself," said Clarice with a shrug. "All the more for me."

Frankly, I'd had my fill already, both from the danger and excitement as well as the food. As I started subjecting myself to an extensive session of grooming, and so did my friends, I suddenly spied two more additions to the roof. They had come up along the service stairs, which deposited the restaurant staff to the roof out of sight from the diners, and if I wasn't mistaken, one of them was actually the woman who had greeted us downstairs: Kirsten Turton. The man she was kissing now wasn't her husband, though, but a swarthy individual with killer good looks and a chef's apron, just like Roger Turton.

"Who's that guy?" I asked.

"That's her husband, of course," said Brutus. "Look at them kissing. They're clearly in love."

Harriet sighed. "So nice when they're still in love after years of marriage, isn't it? So romantic."

Clarice gave the couple a quick glance. "That's not her husband. That's Marco Welling. He's the sous-chef."

Dooley seemed surprised. "But... but that means... that means that..."

Clarice grinned. "I know, right? Mrs. Turton is having an affair."

CHAPTER 34

Odelia was feeling so relieved that she actually felt it as a physical sensation in her body. She had been experiencing a sort of pain in her stomach all day from the tension, and now that Charlene was sitting across from her, she could finally relax, and she felt how tense she had been.

Next to her, Grace was eating from the kids' menu the restaurant offered, and as she assisted her daughter by cutting up her meat, she breathed a sigh of relief that her family was together again, all safe and accounted for.

Charlene had just finished telling them about her harrowing experience, which in the end she had managed to turn around herself. This was such a major feat, and the whole reason she was the mayor of Hampton Cove. Odelia didn't know if she would have the sangfroid to negotiate with her abductors and secure her own release. Though it had to be said that Vale and Carew weren't exactly the kind of tough gangsters they made themselves out to be. At one time, they had even befriended Marge and worked at the library for a while.

Now they would be behind bars and hopefully wouldn't bother them again.

"They really don't seem to learn their lesson, do they?" said Chase, marveling at the sheer stupidity of the criminal duo. "Time and time again they get caught and yet they persist."

"Yeah, they really are the poster boys for recidivism," said Marge. "Though if the parole board suggests they start working at the library again as part of their rehabilitation, I won't say yes this time. No way."

While they worked at the library that time, they had managed to dig a tunnel to the bank next door, abscond with the contents of dozens of safe deposit boxes, and then flee to Mexico.

"So no idea who told them to kidnap you, huh?" said Gran as she studiously worked a lobster to comply with her desire to have a taste.

"No idea," said Charlene. "Though you said it's got something to do with the murder of Alan Gerard, is that correct?"

"Has to be," said Gran. "Sonny is Jerry Vale's brother-in-law, or at least he was before their respective wives divorced them both. And he told us that he was told to go to Alan Gerard's house and find that painting, presumably after Vale and Carew tried to do the same thing and failed, resulting in the death of poor Mr. Gerard."

"That must be one valuable painting," said Scarlett.

"Has to be," Gran confirmed. "Max saw the painting and says it showed sunflowers. And Dooley, who witnessed the crime this morning, also mentioned hearing something about a painting."

"Okay, so our mystery person hired Vale and Carew to find that painting," said Chase, summing things up. "They try to get Alan Gerard to reveal the hiding place of the thing, and he ends up having a heart attack and they flee the scene. So then they go and kidnap Charlene, allegedly because her ex-husband wants to make her reconsider their divorce. And meanwhile, Sonny is hired to find that same painting and he's successful and recovers it from the house, only to drop it off at a pre-arranged place at the park and receive payment for his services."

"So what does Alan Gerard's painting have to do with me?" said Charlene, voicing a question that had been on all of their minds ever since the truth had been revealed to them. "Unless they were going to demand a ransom for me?"

"Vale and Carew denied that," Chase pointed out. "No ransom was ever mentioned, only this business about an ex-husband who wanted one last chance to be reconciled with the woman he loved."

Charlene rolled her eyes. "If only they'd known Jim. He was probably the least romantic person in the world, and happy as a clam when I told him I wanted a divorce."

Jim Hobbin had been cheating on Charlene with another woman, a fellow member of the archery club they both were members of, for many years. Oddly enough, the moment the divorce came through, the mistress broke up with Jim. Apparently, she preferred being his mistress to being his wife.

"Okay, so let's forget about all of that for now," Uncle Alec suggested. His cheeks were red and he hadn't stopped darting the occasional glance at Charlene, as if to make sure his eyes weren't deceiving him and she really was back. His smile was infectious. "Let's just be happy that we're together as a family," he said. "And enjoy each other's company and be grateful for the happy ending." He raised his glass. "Charlene is back, and that's all that counts."

And so they all raised their glasses in a toast to Charlene, who took it all in stride and looked as happy as her partner to have survived this ordeal.

Just then, Odelia thought she saw something big and furry scoot along the wall of the restaurant. One moment it was there, then it was gone. But then loud cries of dismay rang out all across the restaurant, and as she looked up, she saw that more of the furry creatures were traversing the restaurant floor, scooting between chairs and streaking along people's legs. Suddenly, she felt something stroke against her own leg, and she yelled out in surprise and got up so fast her chair tumbled back.

"It's rats!" suddenly, someone screamed. "They're everywhere!"

He was right. All of a sudden, the whole place was filled with hairy creatures who were indeed everywhere. They were crossing the floor, crawling onto tables and attacking the food, jumping over each other in a bid to get to the best bits, and causing people to scream in horror and jump up on tables and chairs to get away from the creatures, which were just about the biggest rats she had ever seen!

And just when complete pandemonium seemed to break out, all of a sudden the largest rat of all appeared, emitted a deafening screech, and attacked the other rats! But when Odelia looked closer, she saw this wasn't a rat. It was Clarice! And as she went after the rats, the creatures seemed to consider their options, and before long, they accepted defeat and ran for the hills—or in this case, the kitchen, where they disappeared as quickly as they had arrived.

All eyes now settled on Clarice, who sat in the center of the restaurant, cool as a cucumber, with a big rat clasped between her teeth. One moment it was there, the next only its tail was visible, as Clarice chugged the whole thing down in one gulp. The tail dangled there, and then, as an afterthought, she swallowed the tail, and the rat was gone.

Applause broke out all around, as the heroics of the formerly feral cat were lauded with an enthusiasm even the restaurant chef's signature dish had never garnered. But then Clarice, true to form, gave a sort of vicious growl and stalked off at a leisurely pace—the coolest cat in the universe. Her work was done.

CHAPTER 35

We were still on the roof when the hubbub broke out. Figuring they were alone, Mrs. Turton and her sous-chef were discussing their future, which they believed would be with each other, and not their respective current partners.

"The moment we get that money," said Mrs. Turton, "we pull the plug and we're done."

"You got it, baby," said Marco. "I pull the plug on my marriage, you pull the plug on yours, and then our bright future awaits. New restaurant, new relationship, the works."

They kissed again, and Dooley looked sad. "But they're not married to each other," he said. "So why are they kissing? It doesn't make sense, Max."

"Sometimes people who are married fall in love with other people," I explained. "And so they divorce the people they're married to and marry the people they're attracted to. It happens, Dooley." He turned to me with a look of dismay. "But... it won't happen to Odelia and Chase, will it? Or to Marge and Tex? Or Uncle Alec and Charlene? They all love each other."

"You never know what will happen in the future," said Clarice, not beating about the bush. But when she saw how upset her words made Dooley feel, she quickly backtracked. "But it's clear to me how much your humans love each other, so I wouldn't worry about anything like that happening to them, Dooley."

Dooley only looked moderately relieved by this. "I really hope so."

"So when are you getting that money?" asked Marco now.

"Soon, baby, soon," said Kirsten.

"I can't wait," he said with a grin.

Which is when suddenly all hell seemed to break loose downstairs. There was loud screaming, tables being overturned, plates and glasses crashing to the floor and chairs toppling over. As Clarice pricked up her ears, a look of the utmost focus came into her eyes. "Rats!" she suddenly hissed. "I can hear rats!"

And before we could stop her, she was already streaking down the stairs at a speed I had never seen any cat travel before. One moment she was there, the next she was gone. Like a flash—or maybe a superhero.

"Did she say rats?" asked Brutus with a look of concern.

"This isn't good," said Harriet. "People don't like it when they see a rat, especially at a five-star restaurant." A look of delight came over her. "You know what this means, though, right? They'll all leave and leave their plates, and there will be even more food for us!"

She might be right in her determination, but for the restaurant owners, this was probably bad news. Like she said, when people go out to dinner, the last thing they want to see is rats navigating between the tables. It spoils the pleasant mood. Humans may be generous to a fault, but not when they're dining out, and especially not when there are rats about. They might hand a tasty morsel to a passing dog or cat, but they definitely draw the line at rats and their ilk. You might call it a prejudice, but they're not crazy about the species.

On the rooftop, diners must have become aware that there was trouble brewing, for one by one, they left their tables and headed down the stairs, proving that Harriet was right about one thing: very soon there would be food aplenty for the likes of us. Though I was more concerned about our humans, who were downstairs and probably suffering through this rat invasion.

And just as I was about to head down the stairs as well, a loud applause broke out. As I hurried to see what was going on, I caught the tail end of Clarice's performance. She wasn't impressed, as was to be expected, and stalked off stage left. It wasn't hard to guess what had happened, for of the rats, there wasn't a single trace.

But then diners all started leaving, directing irate looks at the restaurant's owners, who were trying to stem the flow and appease the baying and rebelling masses. All to no avail, and before long the whole place had emptied out, except for one table where our very own humans sat. As Dooley, Harriet, and Brutus also descended the stairs, we joined them and asked what was going on.

Odelia crouched down and whispered, "The biggest rats I have ever seen," she said. "And there were so many of them. Dozens, maybe even hundreds! But then Clarice came and they all fled. I've never seen anything like it. It was amazing."

"They'll probably close down the restaurant now," I said. "For reasons of health and safety." We all glanced up at Charlene, who probably had a role to play in all of that. And as Roger Turton and his wife also turned to the mayor, she shook her head. For a moment I fully expected her to give them a thumbs-down gesture, like a Roman emperor of old, but instead, she took them apart for a chat.

Marge sighed. "Looks like dinner is over, people."
"Looks like the Hungry Pipe is over," said Gran.
"Oh, no!" said Harriet. "But they can't!"
"Rats," Brutus grumbled.

CHAPTER 36

Odelia certainly had her hands full. People wanted to know what was going on, and with the abduction of the mayor, the death of Alan Gerard, and now a rat infestation at one of the most popular restaurants in town, their hunger for news was insatiable. So Odelia's editor had her working overtime to provide copy on all of those incidents. Meanwhile, Chase was still trying to figure out who the mysterious mastermind could be behind the events that had rocked our town, and so was Uncle Alec, who was on the warpath now that someone had the gall to target his beloved wife.

It also meant that our humans had us working overtime to find out what was going on, but try as we might, we weren't getting very far. Until suddenly, the great breakthrough came. Dooley and I were walking along Main Street, chatting with this cat and that, when we came upon the General Store and found to our surprise that it was closed. No Kingman, no Wilbur Vickery, and most surprisingly of all, a sign on the door that said, 'Closed due to personal circumstances.'

"That has never happened before, has it, Max?" said Dooley, indicating the sign.

"No, except yesterday, when Gran made Wilbur join her on a mission to find Charlene."

"Maybe he's still looking for her," Dooley suggested.

"Unlikely," I said. "He was there when the news broke that Charlene had been found." Or that she had freed herself from the clutches of her abductors.

And since it never hurts to be inquisitive, we decided to find out what was going on. So we approached the matter from a different angle, in this case from the street that runs parallel to Main Street, and where we could gain access to Wilbur's little patch of city garden via a narrow pathway that runs between these houses. It required jumping up onto a wall and then making our way along a narrow ledge, but we didn't mind, as long as we could satisfy our curiosity.

Moments later, we were touching down in Wilbur's little patch of green, which mainly consists of a single tree, a few tufts of grass, and some haphazardly placed paving stones with a bench where the shop owner could rest his weary bones. Back when he was still a smoker, this was where he liked to have an occasional smoke.

We glanced up at the back of the house, but could find no sign of either our friend or his human. And so naturally we ventured inside via the pet flap, that most wonderful invention. The kitchen was empty, and as far as we could tell, Wilbur wasn't in the store making his inventory. We were up the stairs in a heartbeat, but in the living area there was no sign of the duo either. And so we took the stairs to the third floor, and that's when we hit the jackpot: Wilbur was in bed looking wan, with Kingman lying at the foot of the bed, looking unhappy.

When he saw us, he lifted his head in greeting. "Hey, fellas," he said. "What brings you out here?"

"The shop is closed," Dooley pointed out. "The shop is never closed. Why is the shop closed, Kingman?"

"Yeah, and why aren't you outside talking to people?" I asked. And when I say people, of course, I mean cats.

Kingman heaved a sigh. "Wilbur is depressed, and so he doesn't want to get up and open his store."

"And why is that?" I asked. I'd heard of this strange phenomenon of depression, of course, but had never witnessed it firsthand. It smelled funny, I thought. Like old socks and unwashed armpits. And it looked even funnier, as if Wilbur had been struck by a zombifying virus and was partially paralyzed.

"His favorite restaurant was closed down last night by the mayor," said Kingman.

"I didn't know that Wilbur had a favorite restaurant," I said.

"He had. Not to eat at, mind you, but to deliver food to. He was one of the main suppliers to the Hungry Pipe. Vegetables, meat, fish, and whatever else a fine restaurant needs. Wilbur delivered it all, since Roger Turton believed in working with local suppliers. And now that the restaurant is closed, that will mean a big chunk of his income gone. So he's depressed."

"The restaurant will open again," said Dooley. "Isn't that right, Max?"

"Um…" I said. "I wouldn't be too sure about that. These health inspectors don't have a sense of humor, and I'm pretty sure they don't like rats. So chances are that the restaurant will remain closed for the foreseeable future."

"It wasn't just the rats," said Kingman. "There had been other incidents. Hairs found in soup, bird poop being smeared on plates meant for the diners. Roger even told Wilbur that he thought that saboteurs were at work at his restaurant. So it wouldn't surprise me if they're the ones who released those rats last night."

"And did he tell Wilbur who he thought was responsible?" I asked, though I had a pretty good idea who this might be.

"His wife," said Kingman. "Roger figured his wife was having an affair with his sous-chef, and they were working together to make the restaurant go under and blame it all on him as a way to get rid of him. The actual owner of the restaurant isn't Roger, you see, or his wife. The real owner is Kirsten's dad, who's some kind of big-shot investor. He put up the money and he owns both the building and the restaurant. So when they pull the plug on the place, Roger's father-in-law will blame Roger."

"That can't be right," I said with a frown. I remembered the conversation we'd overheard last night between Kirsten and Marco about the money they were banking on. Could it be... "How well does Wilbur know the Turtons?"

"Oh, pretty well. Like I said, he's been doing business with them for a while now. So now that the place is closed, it's a major blow both to Roger but also to Wilbur."

I nodded. "Thanks for the information, Kingman. You've been most helpful."

And as we made our way back down the stairs, he yelled, "Hey, you haven't told me what to do about Wilbur! How do I get him out of bed?"

Unfortunately, I'm not a shrink, so I couldn't give him advice in that department. So I yelled back, "I'll have to get back to you on that!"

And then we were off, since I'd suddenly had an idea.

CHAPTER 37

Harriet stared at their unbidden and frankly unwelcome guest with unveiled hostility. "I don't understand," she said, not for the first time. "You were supposed to fly to Italy. So why didn't you?"

Shanille lifted her shoulders with a touch of embarrassment. "I guess there was a miscommunication. I thought I was traveling to Rome with Father Reilly, while he felt I should stay here at this pet hotel he had selected."

"So you're not going to be a papal cat?"

"I guess not."

For a moment, silence hung heavy in the air, then Brutus cleared his throat. "I'm going outside for some fresh air. Wanna come?"

"Later," said Harriet curtly. First, she needed to get to the bottom of this thing with Shanille. The three of them were in Marge and Tex's place, where Gran had established Shanille as her house guest for the time being—until Father Reilly returned from Rome. *If* he returned, for Shanille still seemed to be laboring under the notion that he would become the next Pope, something the current Pope would probably have a problem with. "Look, I already established myself as the next cat choir conductor. I even appointed three assistants and I'm organizing a trailer and craft services. So you can't just come barging in here and take over."

"I'm not taking over since I never left," Shanille pointed out.

"Okay, so I'm going to pop out for a moment," said Brutus, and when nobody paid him any attention, he slunk off through the pet flap in the kitchen.

"You did leave," Harriet pointed out. "We all heard it. I was there, and so were Brutus, Max, Dooley, and Kingman. You said you were leaving, and then you left. And so now I'm cat choir's conductor and you're not."

"I *thought* I was leaving, but then I didn't," said Shanille, also becoming a little belligerent now. "So I'm still cat choir's official conductor."

"You were going to run some kind of papal cat choir," Harriet reminded her.

"Well, that didn't happen."

"You can say that again."

For a moment, both cats continued to glare at one another. "Okay, if you don't want me here, just say the word, and I'm gone," said Shanille finally. "I don't like to be where I'm not wanted."

"I don't want you here," said Harriet.

"It's not up to you, though, is it? Gran invited me, and she owns this place, not you."

Harriet knew she wasn't going to win this game, but she was still going to give it her best shot. "Gran might have invited you, but we're a democracy, and in a democracy, we all have to agree and put things to a vote. So I'm going to propose to Gran that we put your being here to a vote. And when the majority decides to kick you out, will you leave quietly, or will you have to be escorted out?"

"I won't have to leave, since the majority will confirm Gran's invitation."

The glaring game recommenced, and so when Max and Dooley walked in five minutes later, they found that the tension in the place was so palpable it was like electricity buzzing in the air.

"Max, just the cat I wanted to see," said Harriet. "Shanille here won't leave—though I should probably call her Philomena now—and she even insists she's still cat choir's conductor, even though she resigned to become a papal cat."

"Max, you're a smart cat," said Shanille. "Harriet here thinks she can kick me out while I've been officially invited here as a guest by Gran, who, last time I checked, is still in charge of this place and not Harriet. So can you please tell her to pipe down and do something useful for a change? Like go and boil her head?"

"Can you please tell Philomena that she should fly to Rome and get lost?"

"Can you please tell Harriet that I'm firing her from cat choir?"

"Can you please tell Philomena she isn't the boss of me and that I'm firing her from cat choir. Though on second thought, I don't have to, since she fired herself."

"Can you please—"

"Ho, ho, ho," said Max, holding up his paws and sounding very much like Santa Claus all of a sudden. "Maybe you should both take a moment and think about what you're doing. You're supposed to be friends, and friends don't tell friends to go and boil their heads. Or tell them to fly to Rome and get lost."

"I'm in charge of cat choir now," said Harriet. "Tell her, Max."

"I'm in charge of cat choir," said Shanille. "So tell her, Max."

"Maybe I should be in charge of cat choir," said Dooley as he regarded the scene with interest. "Since you two can't seem to get along."

Max looked up with a glint in his eyes. "Now there's a good idea, Dooley." And then he did the most outrageous thing. "Okay, so from now on, Dooley is in charge of cat choir and you're both fired. Is that understood? And until you can prove that you're both grown-ups and can behave accordingly, he will remain in charge. And now if you'll excuse us, we have an important case to solve."

And with these words, he swept from the room, only to return a moment later. "I almost forgot what I came here for. Have you seen Gran?"

"Out," said Harriet curtly.

"Out where?"

"Out!" she repeated, turning on him with a vicious gleam in her eye.

Max must have gotten the message, for he quickly left the scene.

"I'm the new cat choir conductor," said Dooley, looking surprised. "How about that?" But when Harriet gave him a look that could kill, he quickly followed in his friend's wake.

For a moment, neither of the two frenemies spoke, then Shanille said, "Now look what you've gone and done!"

"*I've* done? What *you've* done, you mean!"

But since there was no point in arguing, since it looked as if they'd both been benched, they decided to take a break and place their heads on their front paws and stare into space, thinking about what could have been if that busybody Max hadn't interfered.

CHAPTER 38

We arrived in the backyard to find Brutus there, looking distinctly unhappy. "What's going on with Harriet?" I asked.

He shrugged. "Do you have to ask? She's unhappy that Shanille didn't leave, like she said she would, and that she won't be the new cat choir conductor after all."

"No, because I'm the new conductor," said Dooley happily.

Brutus gave him an indulgent smile. "Of course you are."

"No, but I am. Max just put me in charge because Harriet and Shanille weren't behaving properly and were calling each other names."

"They were?" said Brutus. "This is worse than I thought." He gave Dooley a commiserative look. "If I were you, I wouldn't accept the position, Dooley. Like the man said, power corrupts, and absolute power corrupts absolutely." And with these words, he traipsed off, looking a little dejected, I thought.

Dooley turned to me. "What did he mean by that, Max?"

"Beats me," I said. "Now where is Gran?"

"What do you need Gran for?"

"I want her to check something for me."

"She saved my life, you know," suddenly a voice piped up. We both looked over and saw that Fifi had joined us. She already looked a lot better than she had the day before, after she had witnessed Alan Gerard's mortal remains.

"Who did?" I asked.

"Well, Gran, of course. She took me to a shrink, and after talking to her for about an hour, I saw the light."

Dooley started at this. "Don't go to the light, Fifi!" he exclaimed. "Never go to the light!"

The little Yorkie smiled an indulgent smile. "I won't, Dooley," she said.

"So you talked to a shrink, did you?" I said.

"I did, yeah. Her name is Doris Twist, and she's a very wise person."

"Where does she live, this Doris Twist?" I asked. "It's just that I think I've got another client for her. You see, Wilbur Vickery is depressed, and it looks as if he could use some professional help."

"Doris is a pet shrink, though," said Fifi. "And last time I looked, Wilbur Vickery wasn't a pet."

"Shrinking is shrinking," I said. "And human psychology is probably not all that different from pet psychology."

"Oh, but it is, Max," said Fifi. "For instance, when I told Doris that I felt bad after I had seen that dead man, she said that death is nothing but a transition from this life to the next. So like a moth casts off its form to become a butterfly, Alan Gerard has cast off his human form to become an angel." She sighed happily as she cast her gaze on a nearby flower. "He's everywhere now. In the trees, in the grass, in the flowers."

Dooley suddenly looked uncomfortable. "Mr. Gerard is in the trees?" he asked, looking up at the closest tree, a hefty specimen planted at the bottom of the backyard. "Are you sure? I don't see him."

"It's just a figure of speech, Dooley," said Fifi. "What Doris means is that the spirits of our dearly departed move to a different plane of existence, but they're never really gone. It's just that we can't see them anymore, but if we really want, we can still feel their presence. It gave me a lot of comfort to know that."

"Okay," said Dooley, though he didn't seem one hundred percent convinced.

"Kurt has also been seeing a shrink, though in his case I'm not sure it's working. Only this morning he said he's going to quit drinking so much coffee, since it's bad for his ticker and he doesn't want to croak like Mr. Gerard did."

"Well, at least he's taking care of his health," I said.

"I guess we all have our lessons to learn," Fifi agreed. She gave me a smile. "When you see Gran, will you thank her for me? She's a real lifesaver."

"I will," I said. First, we had to find her, though.

"She'll probably be at the doctor's office, Max," said Dooley.

And so we decided to set paw for that establishment, hoping to find our human present and accounted for. It didn't take us long to get there, and when we arrived, much to my relief we did see Gran's familiar form seated behind the desk, welcoming Tex's patients and asking them to take a seat in the waiting area. At the moment, the reception area was empty, though, with not a single patient in sight.

"Gran, just the person I wanted to see," I said as we joined her behind that desk. She was playing a game of Scrabble on her computer and gave us a smile.

"That was some fast thinking on Clarice's part last night, wasn't it? She got rid of those rats pretty swiftly. In fact, I don't think I've ever seen anything like it. One moment they were swarming all over that place and the next they were gone. Talk about quick service."

"The thing is, Gran," I began.

"You know, I've been thinking some more about this case, and the more I do, the more I'm convinced that this whole case revolves around Alan Gerard. Someone knew about that painting he had tucked away, and they orchestrated this whole abduction business to keep us all busy looking for Charlene when all the while the crux of the thing was that painting. So it stands to reason it must be someone closely connected to Mr. Gerard. Maybe a relative or a friend." She pointed at me. "That's what you should be looking into, Max. There's your clue."

"I know," I said. "But the thing is—"

"Did Alan Gerard have kids? Did he have a brother or a sister? Maybe an old patient or a colleague from his days as a surgeon? I'm going to tell Chase tonight, and hopefully he'll be able to dig something up."

"Yes, but—"

Just at that moment, the door to the doctor's office swung open, and a man walked in. I recognized him as Roger Turton, and he did not look well. Which, of course, was to be expected if his restaurant was about to go under.

"I've got an appointment with Dr. Poole," he said as he approached the desk.

"Mr. Turton, hi," said Gran pleasantly. "Take a seat, and the doctor will be with you shortly."

He tapped the desk smartly and gave Gran a grateful smile. "You were there last night, weren't you? You and your family?"

"I was, yes," said Gran.

"Then you saw the whole thing. How someone released hundreds of rats in my restaurant and effectively managed to put me out of business."

"You think someone did that on purpose?" asked Gran.

"Absolutely. And I know exactly who's behind it." He glanced left and right, even though he and Gran were the only people in the place. Then he leaned in and lowered his voice in a conspiratorial manner. "I think my wife is having an affair with my sous-chef. And it wouldn't surprise me if he's the one who's been going out of his way to get rid of me. A customer found a hair in his soup the other day, you know. And then someone smeared pigeon poop on the plates just as they were going out to the diners. And now those rats? It's too much of a coincidence."

"But what does he hope to gain by shutting you down?" asked Gran. "If the Hungry Pipe goes out of business, he will lose his job."

"My father-in-law owns the restaurant," said Mr. Turton. "So effectively, it's him they're targeting. He invested a lot of money into that place, and if we go bust, he won't be happy. And who is he going to blame, you think?" He thumped his chest. "Me. He'll figure I betrayed his trust and want me out. Out of the business, out of his life—out of my marriage to his daughter. And then Marco will be waiting in the wings, ready to take over. Take my restaurant and my wife."

"No," said Gran in a low voice. It was almost like an episode from one of her favorite soaps. "Marco wouldn't do that. Would he?"

"Oh, yes, he would. And so would my father-in-law. He's a hard man, and only thinks about the bottom line. Make him lose money and that's it—you're gone. That's how he is in business, and it's the same way he runs his family."

"But surely your wife loves you, Mr. Turton. She wouldn't—"

"Oh, yes, she would. They're having an affair, I'm telling you. The looks, the texts, the smiles when they think I'm not looking. It's obvious they're crazy about each other." And then all of a sudden, he actually burst into tears right then and there!

"Oh, Max, the poor man!" said Dooley.

Gran hurried around the desk and gave the man a pat on the back. "There, there," she said. "Just let it all out. That's a good boy."

The door of the inner office opened and Tex stood there. For a moment, he merely stared at the strange scene of his mother-in-law hugging this man, who stood crying buckets.

"Don't just stand there," Gran said. "Can't you see he's hurting?"

Tex jerked into motion. "Let's get him into my office," he said, and together they assisted the restaurateur into the doctor's office. Moments later, they had sat him down at Tex's desk, and Gran came hurrying out again. Just before the door closed, we could hear Tex say, in his best doctor's voice, "Now what brought this on, Roger?"

"Oh, doctor!" said Roger.

But then Gran closed the door, and the conversation was cut off. Doctor-patient privilege and all of that, I suppose. That's when Gran pressed a button on her phone, and we could follow the conversation between Tex and Roger as if we were in the room. When we gave her a look of astonishment, she shrugged. "In case he gets violent, I have to be in there in a flash. Just a precaution, mind you."

"Of course," said Dooley, nodding. "That's very clever of you, Gran."

Very clever indeed. And that's when I finally told her of my suspicions.

CHAPTER 39

Valerie Markell checked her watch and wondered what was taking Kiki so long. Even though she still didn't fully approve of her associating with this kid Dean, at least according to Sonny the kid wasn't as bad as they had thought he was. Soft-spoken, polite, friendly, and he played basketball. So maybe they had been a little hard on Kiki when they told her not to get involved with him?

Their daughter was a teenager now, and according to all the YouTube videos she had watched and all the online articles she had read, and all of their friends who had teenagers themselves, it was only going to get more and more difficult to control her. The best thing they could hope for was that they'd raised her well and instilled enough proper values in her so she wouldn't go off the rails completely.

In this day and age of the ubiquity of the mobile phone and social media, there was simply no way you could make one hundred percent sure your kids wouldn't get involved with the wrong kind of person. So she was actually grateful that Sonny had taken the trouble to talk to the kid and make sure he wasn't some kind of juvenile delinquent, a drug dealer, or a violent gang member, or whatever.

She stubbed out her cigarette in the ashtray located on the patio table and went inside. It was a habit she had been desperately trying to break, but so far without success. She carefully closed the kitchen door and walked into the living room, her heels making a clickety-clackety sound on the stone floor. She and Sonny had bought this modest little row house, but that was before his life had gone off the rails. She had known going in that he was a crook, of course, but had always hoped he'd be a good crook. A talented one who'd bring home the bacon. When she had finally admitted to herself that he was never going to amount to anything, she had some hard choices to make, but finally decided to move on. Life was too short to be stuck with a loser for a husband, and so she had kicked him out and hadn't regretted the decision one moment, and neither had Kiki.

The girl needed a proper role model. A dad she could look up to and go to for advice. The only advice Sonny liked to dole out was that as long as you still had all your hair, everything else would work out just fine.

Her sister Marlene had suffered a similar ordeal when she married that no-good little weasel Jerry Vale, but at least she had caught on pretty fast and in doing so had set an example for her younger sister. Odd, though, that both sisters would have married similar men. Almost as if there was some kind of genetic predisposition involved, even though their parents were good, hardworking people without a single criminal bone in their bodies.

Marlene was dating the director of their local museum for natural history, a good, kind-hearted man and an upstanding citizen—quite the polar opposite of Jerry. And once again, Valerie had taken a page from her older sister's book and had started dating a fine man herself.

Suddenly, a car pulled to a stop in front of the house, and two people got out: a tall guy who looked like a cop, and a woman who reminded her of that reporter, Odelia Kingsley. But when she looked a little closer, she realized that it was, in fact, Mrs. Kingsley. The four cats traveling in her wake were a dead giveaway. The reporter was famous for being some kind of cat lady, which Valerie had always thought was a funny quirk.

Her heart stopped when she realized that the man actually was Odelia's husband, Chase Kingsley, a police detective. Which could only mean one thing: something had happened to Kiki!

"Oh, God, no," she thought. "Tell me it isn't so." She hurried to open the door even before the duo had reached it, and immediately asked, "Is it Kiki? Did something happen to my daughter?"

The reporter gave her a reassuring smile. "We're not here about your daughter, Mrs. Markell. We are here to inform you that your ex-husband, Sonny Hayworth, was arrested last night on suspicion of breaking into the house of your late uncle, Alan Gerard. Mr. Gerard was your uncle, was he not?"

She nodded, greatly relieved that Kiki was all right. "I know about Sonny," she said as she stepped aside to let the twosome into the house. She watched with a frown on her face as the procession of cats followed in their wake. She wasn't a big fan of cats, but apparently, she had no choice but to allow them access to her home. They had once owned a cat, but unfortunately the animal had proven a disappointment, shedding hair everywhere and creating a real mess. So she had told Sonny to get rid of it and he had, telling Kiki that it had run away. "He called me from the police station last night after he was arrested to ask if I could arrange a lawyer for him. And also, Kiki was there when he was arrested, so she also told me what happened. Sonny stole one of my uncle's paintings, is that correct?"

"That is correct," said Odelia as she looked around the living room. "This is very nice," she said admiringly. "Very spacious and very light. And I like the sunflower theme."

She smiled. "I love sunflowers. They're my favorite flower. If I could, I would plant them everywhere, but Sonny was dead set against it. He hates flowers. Said they smell funny. So when we were still married, I wasn't allowed to buy any. But once we got divorced, I redecorated the entire place and put them everywhere." She gestured to the sofa, which was upholstered in a fine fabric with a sunflower motif. Very bright and very pleasant, like the rest of the house. Even her linens had a sunflower motif, and all of her wallpapers and her curtains, of course.

The cop and his wife took a seat, and for a moment she wondered if she should offer them any refreshments. She wasn't sure what the custom was when cops come to your house to announce that your ex-husband has been arrested. Back in the day when she and Sonny were still married, it had happened often enough, but usually they didn't bother to drop by the house. She had to hear it from Sonny himself when he used his one phone call to let her know he was in the pokey again. She finally decided that maybe she could offer them coffee or tea.

"No, that's fine," said Odelia. "We won't stay long."

"So, your uncle," said the detective. "Were you still in touch with him?"

"Oh, no," she said, taking a seat on the opposite sofa. "Uncle Alan had turned into a recluse. After he was convicted of medical negligence, he got into some kind of funk and locked himself up in that old house of his. It greatly pained my mother, who used to be his favorite sister. She would drop by the house often, but he simply wouldn't answer the door. And then later, he turned to selling encyclopedias for a living, which even at the time was a dying profession. Finally, when he reached retirement age, he never left the house again, I think. I actually hadn't seen him since I was a little girl—only heard rumors about the man."

"What kind of rumors?" asked Odelia kindly.

She wondered where this was going, but then figured that it was all part of the case they were building against Sonny. "Oh, you know, that he only wore one type of socks and that he bought them in bulk from a company in New Jersey who delivered them by the truckload. Same thing with his underwear. Every day he'd pick a fresh pair. Then once a month he'd throw them all in a big metal drum in the backyard and burn them. He was quite the eccentric man, my Uncle Alan."

"Did your mother ever mention a certain painting to you?" asked Detective Kingsley. "A painting of sunflowers, more specifically."

Her throat had suddenly gone a little dry. She shook her head. "Nah, I don't remember her mentioning anything like that. Why?"

"Well, your ex-husband broke into your uncle's house yesterday with the sole purpose of stealing a particular painting. It was a painting by an artist named David Cockney, and it's rumored to be worth three million dollars."

Once again she shook her head. "Sonny and I are divorced, detective. And one of the reasons I divorced him was because of his lack of appreciation for the distinction between mine and thine. So frankly, it doesn't surprise me that he would get himself in trouble with the law again. I've never known it otherwise."

"But this painting—did you know that your uncle had it?"

She shook her head vehemently. "This is the first time I've heard about that painting, detective."

"Are you sure your mother never mentioned it to you?"

"Never. I had no idea. We all thought Uncle Alan was a harmless eccentric but also poor. We thought he lost all of his money when the relatives of that patient who died on his operating table sued him. That lawsuit left him completely broke."

"Oddly enough, the theme of the painting is sunflowers," said Odelia, gesturing to the walls and the myriad real-life sunflowers in vases on every available surface.

She swallowed away a lump. "I guess our love for sunflowers must run in the family. My mother also loved them, and so did my grandmother. So I guess Uncle Alan loved them, too."

"The thing is, Mrs. Markell," said Detective Kingsley, "that someone told your ex-husband to steal that painting. And that same person also told your sister's ex-husband, Jerry Vale, to kidnap Mayor Butterwick. We think that the same person is behind both cases, as in the initial instance, Mr. Vale was actually hired to find that painting. Only he couldn't locate it, and your uncle died while being interrogated about the painting's hiding place. So a second attempt was made, and this time Sonny was successful in retrieving the painting."

"So you managed to get it back?" she asked.

"No, we didn't. Sonny was instructed to drop the painting off at the park in exchange for his fee, and he complied. The person who ordered the theft and also the abduction of Mayor Butterwick is the one we believe currently possesses the painting."

"And who would this person be?" asked Valerie innocently. She should have made them some coffee or tea. And maybe a slice of cake. She had some excellent lemon drizzle cake in the fridge that had such a gorgeous yellow color. Just like a sunflower. Tea and cake always lifted the atmosphere, which she had the impression was becoming decidedly stifling all of a sudden.

"We actually made an arrest this morning," said Odelia. "And my uncle is in the process of questioning this person as we speak."

She stared at the woman. "You arrested the person responsible for my uncle's death?"

"We did. But we believe he wasn't working alone but in conjunction with his girlfriend. Or I should probably say his mistress, as he's a married man."

"Who... who is he?" she asked, her voice awkwardly constrained.

Just then, the cats suddenly reappeared. She hadn't even been aware they were gone. They uttered the kind of sound she hated so much, a mixture of mewling and caterwauling that set her nerves on edge, if they hadn't been there already.

"Could I use your bathroom for a moment?" asked Odelia, getting up.

"Uh, sure. It's down the corridor to the left and then on the right."

The reporter took off, her cats in her wake, and she wondered how anyone could endure being around cats all the time. It would drive her up the wall.

"The thing is, Mrs. Markell," said Detective Kingsley, "that we believe the person our suspect was involved with was you."

She stared at the man. "Me!" she cried.

"That's right. Why else would he have known about that painting that your uncle kept hidden in his attic for so many years? We believe that you told him about that painting and what you thought it might be worth. And we also believe that it was you who put the idea of retrieving the painting from your uncle into his head and set this whole thing in motion."

"I can assure you I have no idea what you're talking about, detective," she said, sitting upright now, her cheeks burning. "It's true that I probably should start dating again—my sister keeps telling me to get on one of those dating apps—but with a teenage daughter to take care of and working full-time, I frankly am not in the mood to invite a man into my life at the moment. Maybe when Kiki is a little older and doesn't give me so much grief." She smiled nervously. "Do you have kids?"

"I do, yes. A daughter."

"How old is she?"

"Three."

"They're adorable at that age, aren't they? But just wait another ten years, and trust me, ten years is nothing. Before you know it, she'll be slamming doors, shouting at you, and generally behaving like a horrible monster. So trust me, I don't have the bandwidth or the energy for a new man in my life right now."

"And yet we think that you have been secretly dating someone, and that same someone is the mastermind behind the theft of your uncle's painting, indirectly responsible for your uncle's death, and also for the abduction of Mayor Butterwick."

"But I don't even know Mayor Butterwick!" she cried, trying to hold on to her equanimity but failing miserably. "Why would I want her kidnapped?"

"Now that wasn't your idea," he said. "That was entirely his. But I'm sure he told you all about it, since you are the one who told him to hire your sister's ex-husband, a man whose criminal antecedents you're very familiar with because of your family ties. And when Vale couldn't deliver the goods, you told your lover to hire your ex-husband instead. Sonny may not have been a good husband, but you knew full well that he has an excellent reputation as a burglar, and he proved you right by laying his hands on that painting and setting you on a path to success."

She stared at the man, deciding that maybe keeping her mouth shut was the best option going forward.

"You see, he needed money so he could divorce his wife and relaunch his business, and you thought you had found the perfect solution. One that would make him as successful as he thought he could be and in a position where he could marry you."

"I think you're barking up the wrong tree, detective," she said. "I'm not involved with any man at the moment, and I didn't know about any painting."

Just then, the detective's wife returned from the bathroom, and as she glanced over to the woman, her jaw dropped when she saw that she was carrying in her arms… her uncle's painting.

"Look what I found," said the reporter. "Stuffed behind your bedroom closet."

Which is when Valerie knew that the gig was up and she might as well tell them everything.

CHAPTER 40

It had been an eventful couple of days, and I think we were all looking forward to returning to life as usual. But most of all, we wanted to celebrate the fact that Charlene had been returned to us unscathed and that all had ended well. And so, Tex took out his grill from the garden house, and with the assistance of his brother-in-law Alec and his son-in-law Chase, fired it up with every intention of treating his family to the perfect meal.

That included no less than six cats and two dogs, who must have instinctively felt that something good was coming and had joined us for this occasion. And so, that Saturday afternoon found me, Dooley, Harriet and Brutus on the porch swing, but also Clarice and Shanille, and of course Fifi and Rufus. On the human side, we had Chase and Odelia, Grace, Marge and Tex, Gran and Scarlett, and Uncle Alec and Charlene. All in all, a full house! And since Charlene felt appreciative of all the efforts we had gone through to secure her safe release, she had decided to offer a glass of champagne in lieu of the root beer and other refreshments usually on offer at these informal occasions.

We had to forego the champagne since cats are all members of the AA, but we did get an extra treat in the form of some delicious liver pâté Charlene had brought. We had, after all, been more than helpful in resolving not one but two cases, even though they were related.

"I didn't know you were staying here, Shanille," said Rufus.

"She isn't," said Harriet. "She's supposed to be in Rome."

"Let's not get into all of that again," I suggested.

Harriet shrugged. "Just one dig should be allowed."

"Okay, so you had your one dig. Now let's drop the subject."

"Okay, Max," said Harriet with an expressive eye roll. "If you say so."

"Have you heard from Father Reilly?" asked Brutus.

"I have," said Shanille. "Well, not me personally, of course. But he did call Gran and told her that his visit is going well so far. He still hasn't met the Pope, though, since as it turns out the Pope is actually in Africa and won't be back until the week after Father Reilly flies back to the States."

"Looks like he didn't coordinate his schedule with that of the Pope," I said.

"No, he probably should have called His Holiness and compared schedules. But he said Rome is a beautiful city and he's meeting lots of old friends and having a great time. And then he actually asked about me!"

"Of course he did," I said. "Because he cares about you."

"He did put me in that pet hotel," said Shanille. "Which made me wonder if maybe I should go and pick a new human. But as he explained to Gran when she quizzed him on that decision, he didn't want to impose on anyone, and he had read some very good reviews about that particular pet hotel, so he thought I'd have a great time surrounded by friends and being pampered."

"Well, you are staying with friends and you are being pampered," Dooley pointed out.

Shanille smiled. "Yeah, I guess so." She darted a quick look at Harriet. "At least the pampering part is true."

"Oh, don't be like that," said Harriet, giving the choir conductor a nudge. "I'm sorry I was so upset, okay? I was disappointed, that's all, since I figured I was going to lead cat choir from now on. But I'm over it now, so I'm fine with it."

"You could be *my* assistant," Shanille suggested.

"You mean like turn your pages?" asked Harriet.

We all laughed, since Shanille doesn't actually use a music score when she conducts cat choir. She does it all 'au naturel,' so to speak.

"Okay, so now please don't keep us in suspense any longer, Max," said Fifi. "Who abducted Charlene and why? And how did you catch him?"

"Why, Roger Turton, of course," said Brutus. "Isn't it obvious?" But then he gave me a grin. "Just kidding. How did you figure it out, Max, cause I had no clue."

"Well, the thing that put me on track to figuring it out was when Kiki revealed that her mother was dating a man whose cooking skills were superior to those of her dad. An actual pro, she called him. It made me wonder if there could be a connection between what was going on at the Hungry Pipe, with the sabotage and everything, and the kidnapping and the home invasion at Mr. Alan Gerard's house. A little digging soon revealed that Mr. Gerard was, in fact, Valerie Markell's uncle, and it wasn't a big leap to implicate her in this whole nasty business. And then of course there was the cigarette," I said, with a nod to Dooley.

"I knew that was an important clue!" said Dooley.

"I think Mr. Gerard felt he didn't have long left to live, and he wanted to make peace with his family, who he had pushed away over the years. So he invited his niece to pay him a visit, and during that visit the topic of sunflowers cropped up, since Valerie was wearing a dress with a sunflower motif. So he happened to mention that he owned a painting by an artist named David Cockney with that exact same motif, and even though it didn't ring a bell at the time, when she got home she googled the name and discovered the painting's value. Alan Gerard had once treated Mr. Cockney as a patient years ago, back when the latter was a struggling young artist, and since he had no money to pay for the operation had offered one of his paintings instead, which Mr. Gerard kept in his attic, figuring it wasn't worth a great deal of money. Since then of course David Cockney has become a household name, with his paintings selling for millions a piece."

"And the day Valerie paid a visit to her uncle she smoked a cigarette," said Brutus, nodding.

"She did, yeah. Chase finally had it examined and traces of Valerie's DNA were found on that cigarette. So her story about not having seen or spoken to her uncle since she was a child were a lie. They had met, and when she mentioned the Cockney painting to her lover, that's when they formed a plan to steal it. And when Johnny and Jerry didn't deliver the goods, and in fact made a mess of things by not only precipitating her uncle's heart attack but also hitting that girl while they were making their getaway, she turned to her ex-husband Sonny."

"But why, Max?" asked Dooley. "Why would Valerie want her uncle dead?"

"She didn't want him dead. She wanted that painting found so she could sell it for three million dollars and fund the kind of lifestyle she had always dreamed of. One of the reasons she divorced Sonny was that he was a pretty small-time crook without any ambition to move beyond the petty crime he was good at. She wanted more out of life. Bigger and better. And when she met Roger Turton, she found in him a kindred spirit, because Roger wasn't happy with his lot in life either."

"But he had everything," said Harriet. "A successful restaurant, a wonderful and supportive wife. What else could he wish for?"

"Independence," I said. "Roger wasn't happy that his father-in-law controlled the purse strings. It was Kirsten's father's money that had set up the business when he invested in the restaurant, and so Roger felt as if he was in his father-in-law's employ. He wanted to be his own man. And so when Kirsten started an affair with Roger's sous-chef Marco, he felt that enough was enough. Not only was his father-in-law in charge of every financial aspect of the restaurant, but now his wife was cheating on him. So when he met Valerie and they got to talking, they soon discovered they shared a mutual interest in getting more out of life. And from that shared dream, they soon started making plans."

"They could have waited for her uncle to die of natural causes," Shanille said. "She would have inherited everything and there would have been none of this nastiness."

"Not exactly," I said. "Valerie isn't the only relative Alan Gerard had. There's Valerie's sister Marlene, but also other aunts and uncles and assorted family members. The estate would have had to be divided between all of them, and that's without knowing what was in his will. Maybe he had decided to leave everything to charity, or to the company who delivered his socks. Valerie did mention he was an eccentric. So they couldn't take that chance. Instead they decided to go for the gold and get their hands on that painting now, so Roger could buy himself a new restaurant."

"So who was behind that sabotage at the Hungry Pipe?" asked Brutus.

"Roger himself," I said. "He wanted to destroy his father-in-law's business and then buy it back from him at a reduced price and really be his own boss. He was going to divorce Kirsten, kick out Marco, and set himself up in business with Valerie by his side. It didn't hurt that he could blame the sabotage on Marco and Kirsten, sowing seeds of resentment in his wife's family."

"And what about the abduction?" asked Harriet.

"When Roger relaunched the Hungry Pipe, there were a lot of hoops he had to jump through. A lot of administrative stuff he had to battle, since the building wasn't up to code and Town Hall gave him a really hard time. And it didn't end there. Generally, he felt that Charlene's administration was making things way too hard for the local business community, and he wanted to teach her a lesson. It would also serve as a distraction from the home invasion at Alan Gerard's."

"So he never had any intention of demanding a ransom for Charlene?"

"No, he didn't. He just wanted to punish her for treating him in a way that he felt was unfair and damaging to his ambitions as a businessman and restaurateur."

"Wow, if every local businessman is going to start abducting politicians because they don't agree with the way they're being treated, it's going to get very interesting," said Rufus. "And not very pleasant for those local politicians!"

"I think Roger Turton is an extreme case," I said. "After years of hard work, it looks as if he suddenly snapped and made some very ill-advised decisions."

"What's going to happen to Kiki now?" asked Fifi. "Now that both her mom and her dad are in prison?"

"She'll go and live with Valerie's sister Marlene," I said.

"Jerry Vale's ex-wife," Harriet pointed out.

"That's right."

"Let's hope Kiki will stay on the straight and narrow," said

Brutus. "With a family like that, she might be tempted to go down the same road."

"I doubt that very much," I said. "You can always determine your own path yourself, and not let it be determined by the path others have traveled, even if they are your parents. So in that sense, I think she will be just fine."

"Too bad the Hungry Pipe is closed down for business," said Clarice. "I wouldn't mind going there for dinner every night. Those rats were particularly big and juicy."

We all shivered at these words. "I don't get it," said Shanille. "They had the best food on the menu, and you still preferred to have rats for dinner?"

Clarice shrugged. "Natural, unprocessed foods, Shanille. That's what it's all about. If I were you, I would put fresh rat on the menu every night. In fact, if you want, I could go out right now and fetch you a nice specimen. Will do you a world of good. What do you say?"

"No, thanks," said Shanille with a shiver. "I'm good."

"Suit yourself," said Clarice. "It's your funeral."

"More like the rats' funeral," Brutus murmured.

"So how are you feeling now, Fifi?" asked Dooley.

"Oh, I'm fine," said Fifi.

Rufus looked up at this. "Why? What's wrong?"

"Fifi wasn't feeling well after she saw Mr. Gerard," I explained. "But then Gran took her to a pet shrink, and she's already feeling a lot better—aren't you, Fifi?"

"I went back to that same shrink, and she gave me some more good advice, and I think I've put that whole episode past me now. It's all about the light, see."

And as she repeated her earlier story about going to the light, I saw Dooley having a hard time containing his admonition to never go to the light.

The food had arrived, and I was relieved to find that it

wasn't fresh rat on the menu, as no doubt Clarice would have preferred, but lamb chops and chicken wings, cooked to perfection by the trio of chefs manning the grill. We all got our share and dug in with relish, as did the human contingent. And so for a few moments, all conversation ceased while we relished this most sacred of rituals: enjoying a meal in the company of our friends and family, still the best time one can have.

And we had just finished our first batch of delicious goodies when a familiar figure stuck his head around the corner of the house. It was Wilbur Vickery, and the shopkeeper was accompanied by Kingman.

"I'm sorry to bother you," said Wilbur, who looked even worse than the last time we had seen him. "But could I ask you for a small favor?"

"Wilbur!" said Gran, greatly concerned to see her friend in such a state. "What happened to you?"

"Oh, you know," said Wilbur as he approached the gathering. "I just wondered if that shrink you told me I should see—do you have her phone number? I seem to have lost it."

He could have called, of course, but I had the impression that the poor guy was mostly in need of some company. And so a chair was pulled up and the shop owner was told to sit down. An extra plate was put on the table, and before long everyone was fussing over him and making sure that his plate was filled with some delicious provisions and that he ate every single ounce of it.

"Wilbur still not all right?" I asked.

Kingman, who had jumped up onto the porch, which was getting pretty crowded at this point, shook his head sadly. "He's taking the closing down of the Hungry Pipe pretty hard. I keep telling him that things will be all right, but it was a big part of his business, after all. Also, he doesn't listen to a word I say."

"There will be other restaurants," Shanille assured him. "And besides, the General Store is such a fixture in Hampton Cove, word will go out that Wilbur needs help to tide himself over the disappearance of the Hungry Pipe, and solidarity will play its part. Just you wait and see."

"Yeah, Gran and Scarlett will organize a rally or something," said Brutus. "They're good at that kind of thing."

We watched as the color came back to Wilbur's cheeks, and he already looked a lot better than he had before. The fact that Scarlett was sitting next to him and fussed over him like a mother hen probably had a lot to do with that.

"He also misses Father Reilly," Kingman intimated. "He is his best friend, after all. And with him going off to Rome and all, I guess he feels a little lonely."

"Father Reilly will be back soon," I said.

"If he doesn't become the next Pope," said Dooley. He turned to Shanille. "Isn't that right, Shanille? He wants to become the next Pope, doesn't he? And then he will live in Rome for the rest of his life?"

Shanille smiled. "I very much doubt he'll be the next Pope. I think I was a little hasty in assuming that. Only cardinals become popes, and Francis is just a regular priest. As far as I know he'd have to become a bishop first and then an archbishop and then a cardinal. And frankly, I don't think any of that is in the cards. Nor does he have any ambition in that department, if I'm absolutely honest."

"But I thought you wanted to be a papal cat," said Harriet.

Shanille gave her a look of embarrassment. "I just said that to rile you up, Harriet. I know how much you like to be the center of attention, so I figured this would get your goat up."

Dooley laughed. "Harriet is a cat, not a goat!"

Harriet gave Shanille a stern look. "Of course I don't want you to become a papal cat, Shanille. And do you know why?

Because then you'd go and live in Rome, and I would have to miss my friend."

Shanille seemed touched by this. "You would actually miss me?"

"Of course! I mean, who else would I bicker with all the time?"

We all laughed at this.

"It's true," said Shanille. "You're my favorite frenemy, and if I couldn't bicker with you on a daily basis, that would make me very sad indeed."

Dooley didn't seem to get this. "But I never bicker with Max, and he's my best friend. So do you mean we should bicker more? Because I don't want to bicker more. If Max and I would bicker all the time, that would make *me* very sad."

Harriet gave him a peck on the cheek. "Oh, Dooley. Don't ever change."

Dooley blushed as he touched his cheek. "I-I'll do my best not to change."

More food was put on our plates, and the mood turned mellow as our humans discussed the case before turning to the state of the world, and I tuned out.

Who cares about the state of the world when you can enjoy a nice meal with friends? The world could take care of itself—that's my philosophy, and I'll stick to it. Before long, I placed my head on my paws—which is another important part of my philosophy of life: nap time is sacred—and was happily dozing.

"Max?"

"Mh?"

"Do you think we should see a shrink?"

"Now why would we go and see a shrink, Dooley?"

"Oh, I don't know. Fifi seems very happy with hers."

"Fifi lived through a traumatic experience and she needed professional help to process it. We're fine, Dooley. No trauma anywhere on the horizon as far as I can tell."

"Oh, but there is, Max. A big trauma."

"And what is that?" I asked, yawning.

"I still haven't been able to find you a pipe."

I grinned. "That's all right, Dooley. I don't need a pipe."

"But it's Sherlock's pipe, Max. The greatest detective that ever lived. And since you're also a great detective, you deserve that pipe."

"It's fine."

"But I want you to have it."

"Don't sweat it, buddy. And besides, like I already told you, I don't smoke."

Dooley thought for a moment. "So then what can I give you for your birthday, Max?"

"I don't need a birthday present. I've got everything I need right here. And most importantly: I've got the best friend in the world in you."

Dooley sniffed, and when I opened one drowsy eye, it was clear he was actually sobbing.

"What's wrong?" I asked.

"Oh, Max. That's so sweet of you to say!"

"Well, it's the truth. And now let me sleep, will you? I feel a really great nap coming on, and I don't want to stand in its way."

And so we both fell asleep, and so did the rest of the company. Sharing a meal with friends is great, but you know what's even better? Sharing a nap.

It might even beat seeing a shrink, but that could just be me.

THE END

Thanks for reading! If you want to know when a new Nic Saint book comes out, sign up for Nic's mailing list: nicsaint.com/news

EXCERPT FROM PURRFECT STORM (MAX 77)

Chapter One

Terrence Dallas had traveled over a hundred miles and still hadn't arrived at his destination. So he checked the GPS on his phone again and wondered if he had taken a wrong turn somewhere. His internet connection was spotty, so it wouldn't surprise him if the mellifluous voice was leading him astray—deep into the hinterland of whatever town he was passing.

The rain was coming down hard now, preventing him from seeing more than a couple of yards in front of him, his wipers working overtime and still having a difficult time dispensing with the relentless downpour. All of a sudden, lightning flashed on a sign located by the side of the road that announced that he was entering Hampton Cove. Finally. He knew he'd get there eventually. And he had traveled another mile or so when something hard and heavy hit his car from the passenger side and bounced off.

Immediately he stomped on the brakes, and the car skidded to a full stop. For a moment he just sat there, dark-

EXCERPT FROM PURRFECT STORM (MAX 77)

ness all around and no sound but the steady drum of the heavy rain on the roof of the vehicle. He then glanced over to the right side, hoping to see what he might have hit—or, to be more exact: what had hit him. But it was like looking into a dark pit.

For a moment he wavered. Getting out in this deluge seemed inadvisable, to say the least. But he couldn't just continue driving as if nothing had happened. At the very least, he could be guilty of fleeing the scene of an accident, and possibly whatever had hit him—possibly a deer or some other animal crossing the road—was ailing and in urgent need of help.

And so he made a swift decision and opened the car door. Covering his head with his arm and squinting against the rain that was already soaking him to the skin, he hurried around the back of the car to see what he might find. It was as he had expected: a deer had crossed the road at the wrong time, and their destinies had collided, with potentially devastating consequences for the deer.

It was a small specimen, and it was still alive, though even in the faint glow of his brake light, he could see that things didn't look good for the poor creature. And so he did what any person with a heart for the animal kingdom would do: he opened the trunk of his car and carefully placed the wounded deer in there, covering it with a blanket as he did.

Then he got back into his car and entered the word 'vet' into his GPS app. After a few tense moments, the address popped up, and as he put the car in gear, he hoped the vet would be able to save the creature. With a conscience like his, already burdened with numerous transgressions, the last thing he needed was to have the death of Bambi added to the long list.

It didn't take him more than ten minutes to find the place he was looking for, and as he pulled the car to a stop, he saw that the vet worked in a regular house that didn't look like a vet's practice at all. Then again, possibly she worked from home, as a lot of small business owners did. And so he got out, lifted the poor deer from the trunk of his car, and carried it over to the house in question.

For a moment, he wavered. Should he ring the bell or not? Should he risk exposing himself and his business to this person or not? Finally, he decided against it. And so he simply placed the deer on the doorstep, pressed the bell once, and hurried away again.

From the safety of his car, he saw that the door was being opened, and an old lady appeared. This must be the vet, he thought. Along with her, a tall man also joined, and a second, younger woman. The trio stood there for a few moments, looking down at the wounded deer, then glanced up and down the street. But when they failed to locate the person who had delivered the animal to their home, they took the deer inside and closed the door again.

With a smile of satisfaction, Terrence started up the car again and continued his journey. Even if what he was about to do condemned his soul to hell, at least he had done one good thing in his cursed life.

Chapter Two

Dooley had been playing with a ball of wool on the carpet, with Grace cheering him on. For some reason, they both derived a great deal of enjoyment from the procedure. Dooley hit the ball of wool with his paw. It then rolled underneath the couch, from where he retrieved it before recommencing the entire procedure from the beginning.

I watched it all from the safety of the couch, my eyelids growing quite heavy. And after I had watched the scene about half a dozen times, it proved the perfect soporific, and

EXCERPT FROM PURRFECT STORM (MAX 77)

I dozed off. And so it was with some reluctance that I returned to the land of the wakeful when there was an urgent tap on the sliding glass door.

Odelia and Chase, who had been sitting on the couch next to me, watching something on television that proved riveting to them but not so much to me, looked up in alarm.

Standing at the sliding glass door was Odelia's dad, who was waving now and shouting something I couldn't quite comprehend.

And so Odelia got up and opened the door for him.

"A deer," he said once he had stepped inside and shook the moisture from his person.

It was raining hard, the water really coming down in vertical sheets.

"A dear what?" asked Odelia, giving her father a look of concern.

Tex, who was slightly panting, even though the distance from his place to ours is only about ten meters or so, tried again. "Someone dropped off a deer!"

"A dear what, Dad?" Odelia asked, directing a worried look at her husband, who had also joined them. "A dear... patient? A dear... friend? What?"

"A deer!" said Tex, gesticulating a little wildly now. "And it's wounded, and I don't know the first thing about..." He caught himself. "That's not entirely true. I do know a thing or two about veterinary science, but not enough to know what's wrong with the animal. As far as I can tell, it was hit by a car, but we need an actual vet to determine the injuries it has sustained." He took another breath and wiped the rain from his face. "Could you drive us, Chase? My car is in the garage, and Marge's Peugeot isn't big enough to accommodate an animal this size."

Finally, understanding seemed to dawn on both Odelia

EXCERPT FROM PURRFECT STORM (MAX 77)

and Chase. "You mean someone dropped off an actual deer?" asked Chase.

Tex stared at him. "That's what I said. A deer. So could I borrow your truck? Or maybe you could drive? It's just that —I've tried calling Vena, and she's not picking up, so I figured we might as well drive over there. Maybe she went to bed early."

"Or maybe she's not home," Odelia suggested.

"Vena is always home," I said. "She doesn't want to miss out on the opportunity to torture more pets."

My words were lost in the general flow of conversation, and so it was decided that Chase would drive, and Tex would accompany him to the vet with the deer. And since I think we were all curious to see this deer with our own eyes, before long we followed the good doctor into the backyard, through the opening in the hedge, and then inside where it was nice and cozy and comfy, and where we found Marge and Gran standing next to the deer in question.

It was as Tex had indicated: it looked pretty beat up, the poor creature. And so when I asked what happened, at first it didn't even have the strength to respond. Finally, it opened one eye and gave me a searching look. Then it said, "Tell me where I am, please, cat."

"You're in Hampton Cove," I said, "at the home of Marge and Tex Poole, where you were delivered by a person or persons unknown, possibly after you were hit by a car."

"Oh, I was hit by a car, all right," said the deer as it grimaced. "Not a pleasant experience, I can tell you that. My head hurts," it added after a pause. "Ouch."

"We're going to take you to the vet," I explained. "So hang in there, all right? What's your name, by the way? I'm Max."

"Coco," said the deer, quite to my surprise, I won't conceal.

"Okay, Coco, that big man over there is going to lift you

EXCERPT FROM PURRFECT STORM (MAX 77)

up and carry you to his car, and then we're on our way to see the doctor, all right?"

"Fine with me," said Coco. She then gave me a weak smile. "You're coming, too?"

"Well, I guess I could come," I said. I hadn't really thought about it, but when I directed a look at Odelia, she nodded. "Good idea, Max. You can talk to him—or her—so you can make sure it understands what's going on and keep it relaxed."

"It's a her," I said. "And her name is Coco."

"Coco?"

"That's what she said."

And so it was decided: Chase would drive the truck, with Tex to make sure the medical element was covered until we could put Coco in the safe hands of an actual veterinarian, and I would tag along to provide translation services.

"Careful now," said Marge as Chase lifted the deer into his arms. It was a smallish animal, so still very young, I would have guessed, otherwise he probably wouldn't have been able to lift her—some of these deer do grow up to be very big.

Before long, we were riding in the car, with the deer in the bed of the truck, covered with a tarp against the pouring rain, and I wondered how I had managed to get roped into paying a visit to Vena when I could have been home taking a nap.

She is, after all, possibly my least favorite person in the whole wide world, and if I can avoid being anywhere near her, I will. But this was bigger than my personal safety. There was a life at stake here—and so I put my qualms aside and hoped we'd be able to save poor Coco's life.

Chapter Three

Dooley had been playing with a ball of wool when he

suddenly noticed that everyone seemed to have left. He wasn't all that big on playing with balls of wool, but Grace seemed to enjoy it, so he did it as a way of entertaining the little girl.

"Go, Dooley, go!" she said as he gave that ball a nice big thump with his paw that made it skip and hop across the floor until it bumped against the far wall.

And so he ran after it, sliding on the floor as he did until he was the one bumping into the wall.

Grace clapped her hands with glee, which made him feel like a circus performer who has just pulled off the greatest and most difficult stunt. He looked up to see if Max had seen him, which is when he noticed for the first time that of his friend there was no trace. And as he returned to Grace, he saw that of Odelia and Chase there was not a single trace either!

"Where have they all gone?" he asked.

"Beats me," said Grace, holding up her hands in a cute gesture. "Maybe they had something very important to do?"

"But what could be more important than spending the evening together watching television and being together as a family?" he said.

"Grandpa Tex was here," Grace said. "And he said something about a dear... something. And then they suddenly all got up and hurried out, so this dear whatever must be very important."

Dooley's heart sank. A dear whatever had shown up, and they had suddenly all forgotten about him—even Max hadn't bothered telling him he was stepping out for a moment.

"Well, looks like it's just you and me, kid," said Grace, taking it all in stride. "So what are we going to do, huh? Now that we've got the whole house to ourselves? We could have a party, invite some of my friends—or your friends—and really make it count."

EXCERPT FROM PURRFECT STORM (MAX 77)

"On a night like this?" he said, gesturing to the window where the rain was still coming down in rivulets.

"What better way to dispel the gloom from a rainy evening than by having a party?" Grace argued. "Put on some great music, bring out the popcorn and the fizzy drinks, and tread the measure on the dance floor. So let's go, daddyo!"

Dooley had no idea what the toddler was talking about, but he couldn't deny that her enthusiasm was infectious, so he figured he might as well go with the flow. "So who do you want to invite to your party?"

"Well, we could invite all of my friends from the daycare, for one thing."

"Do you have their number?" asked Dooley, who had learned from Max that it's important always to be practical about these things.

Grace's face fell. "I don't even own a phone, Dooley, so how do you expect me to have their number?"

"Without their number, you can't call and invite them," he pointed out.

She thought about this for a moment, but if he thought that the lack of a phone would have put a damper on her plans to have a party, he was very much mistaken. "So let's go and invite them personally," she suggested. "I know where they live. Well, at least some of them, since Mom sometimes drops them off at home."

"I really would rather not go out in this storm," he said. He hated getting wet, and he had a feeling that if he stepped outside of their warm and cozy home, he would get very wet very quickly.

"Yeah, I guess you're right," sighed Grace, who had crawled down from the couch and toddled over to the window. "It is very wet outside, isn't it? And also, I'm not sure my friends will be allowed to go out after dark. Their parents are probably a lot stricter than mine." But then her face lit up with a smile. "Ooh, I know what we can do. We can invite all of *your* friends to drop by. You have a lot of friends, don't you?"

That was true enough. In fact, he had so many friends he didn't even remember all of their names. That's what you got when you were a member of the hottest social group in town. Cat choir might have started as a way to practice their musical skills, but over time it had turned into a social gathering, with music as an excuse to shoot the breeze and hang out. Though in this weather, he would be very much surprised if even a single cat showed up. Like him, most of his friends hated getting wet, and they'd probably all be home right now, making sure to stay warm and dry and, most importantly, safe.

He explained all this to Grace, and as he had expected, the information did not go over well.

"But then who are we going to invite to our party!" she demanded.

"Well, we could invite Harriet and Brutus," he suggested, knowing they were only a hop and a skip away, probably lying on the couch with Gran and Marge and Tex next door. "Or we could invite Fifi or Rufus," he added, referring to their neighboring dogs. "Or if you really wanted to, we could invite Molly and Rupert. I know they live in Blake's field, and they'd be more than happy to join our party."

"Sounds great," said Grace. "Invite them, and let's get this party started!"

And so, despite Dooley's misgivings about venturing out in that terrible downpour, he decided that maybe she was right and that a nice party would lift their spirits and alleviate that sense of ennui that occasionally seemed to come over the kid, and he stuck his head through the pet flap.

For a moment, he stayed on the safe confines of the back terrace, where he was still protected from the worst of the

EXCERPT FROM PURRFECT STORM (MAX 77)

storm by the roof eaves. But then he took a deep breath and streaked across the back lawn until he reached the rose bushes where Harriet and Brutus liked to spend most of their time. He then jumped the fence and down again on the other side. Before long, he was traversing the field, which was almost like a jungle after years of neglect, and called out, "Molly! Rupert! Where are you guys!"

But if he thought that his calls would magically bring out the mice, he was very much mistaken. It actually took him a little while to get any response from anyone at all. In fact, until he had reached the one structure that was still standing in that large field: a derelict old ramshackle shed, where he found shelter from the storm, he hadn't met anyone. He shook off the water drops that had settled on his fur and looked around. It certainly was a little spooky, he thought, with lots of strange sounds and smells that he did not like one bit. As he took another sniff, he determined that the shed had probably been used in recent times as accommodation for a person of the human species. He saw a makeshift cot in the corner of the shack, covered with an old blanket, and he also saw a portable gas burner with a pot placed on top that contained some kind of meal consisting of white beans and tomato sauce, a can lying next to it that had provided this gourmet meal.

And as he sniffed around further, wondering if this could be where Molly and Rupert and their offspring could be hiding, suddenly he was grabbed by a powerful hand, and as he uttered a squeak of surprise, the world suddenly went dark.

ABOUT NIC

Nic has a background in political science and before being struck by the writing bug worked odd jobs around the world (including but not limited to massage therapist in Mexico, gardener in Italy, restaurant manager in India, and Berlitz teacher in Belgium).

When he's not writing he enjoys curling up with a good (comic) book, watching British crime dramas, French comedies or Nancy Meyers movies, sampling pastry (apple cake!), pasta and chocolate (preferably the dark variety), twisting himself into a pretzel doing morning yoga, going for a run, and spoiling his big red tomcat Tommy.

He lives with his wife (and aforementioned cat) in a small village smack dab in the middle of absolutely nowhere and is probably writing his next 'Mysteries of Max' book right now.

www.nicsaint.com

Printed in Great Britain
by Amazon